THRICE
UPON A
MARIGOLD

THRICE
UPON A
MARIGOLD

Jean Ferris

HARCOURT CHILDREN'S BOOKS
Houghton Mifflin Harcourt
Boston   New York   2013

Harcourt Children's Books is an imprint of
Houghton Mifflin Harcourt Publishing Company.

www.hmhbooks.com

Text set in Minister Std Light

Library of Congress Cataloging-in-Publication Data is available.
ISBN 978-0-547-73846-8

Manufactured in the United States of America
DOC 10 9 8 7 6 5 4 3 2 1
4500400783

For E.J., with love from Mimi

1

It wasn't every day that the citizens of the kingdom of Zandelphia-Beaurivage woke up to such startling news from the town crier. Usually what they heard was whose cows had gotten out, or who had found someone else's lost shovel, or the fact that it was raining, when anyone who had eyes could see this for themselves.

But that morning the crier had plenty of news.

"Good morning, citizens! At last the news that we have all been waiting for! It's a girl for Queen Marigold and King Christian! Her name is Princess Poppy Allegra April Rosemary and she arrived at 11:20 last night. The new grandfathers, retired King Swithbert and the troll Edric, will treat everyone to mead and larks' tongues all day today in the castle courtyard! The nursery has been transformed into a bower of yellow—Queen Marigold's favorite color—and purple, King Christian's favorite! This might not be to everyone's taste, but royal personages are not like the rest of us!" (Sometimes the crier got off on tangents.) "Personally, I would have preferred green, but nobody ever asked me! I'm sure that at some point I will be able to announce the date for the Welcome Party, but worrying about that right now is premature!"

He cleared his throat.

"In other news, Farmer Dudley's cows got out early this morning and consumed half of Farmer Eldon's haystack! Farmer Eldon is seeking recompense—preferably in the form of one of the cows who is now carrying around his hay in her stomach!

"Looks like another chilly day, but spring is on the way and soon we should be able to take off the woolen long johns we've been wearing all winter!

"Stay tuned for more announcements!"

He rang his bell, signaling the end of his newscast.

Some days later, Phoebe stood at the leaded-glass window of the library, watching the festivities in the town square. She was sure she was the only subject of Queen Marigold and King Christian who wasn't out there celebrating the long-awaited arrival of the baby princess. But it couldn't be helped. Given her own fearsome history as the daughter of Boris, the exiled torturer-in-chief of the kingdom of Zandelphia-Beau-rivage, Phoebe kept to herself.

She turned away from the window and went back to cutting sheets of paper into thin strips. The cutting tool had been invented by some clever person over in the blacksmith shop and had made her task much eas-ier than when she'd had to use the clumsy short-bladed scissors. The strips were essential for the kingdom's communication by p-mail, as they fit into the cylinders on the legs of the carrier pigeons. The volume of p-mails was increasing every year, and had spread to so many neighboring kingdoms that there was a shortage of trained pigeons and a constant demand for the p-mail paper that the library supplied. It was ironic that

Phoebe, the one responsible for providing the paper for so many p-mail messages, had no one to send any p-mails to.

She was filling the supply basket outside the library door with the paper strips when a young man came striding around the corner, startling her so that she upset the basket.

"Sorry," he said. "I didn't think there'd be anybody here." He bent to help her gather up the spilled strips. "I thought everybody would be out there, as they've been for days now. Jubilizing."

Jubilizing? Phoebe thought. She'd never heard anyone use that word before, and she believed that she, the court librarian, knew more words than anybody else in the kingdom.

She gave the young man a closer look; he was familiar, though she couldn't quite place him. "Of course I'm here. I'm the librarian. Why aren't *you* out there?"

"Oh," he said. "Well, I'm not—I mean, it's so—oh, you know . . ." He trailed off, leaving her as uninformed as before.

"All right, then," she said briskly. "What can I do for you?"

"Oh. Well. I need a book."

"I would say you've come to the right place," she said. "But why now if you thought no one would be here?"

"Oh, that. Well, I just took a chance, I guess. I wasn't going to take the book without permission or anything like that. I just hoped someone would be on duty. And there wouldn't be any lines."

"There are never lines, I'm afraid. Our kingdom hasn't been much for reading books ever since p-mail got so popular. Now, I'll need a little more information if I'm going to be able to help you." It came out more brusquely than she had meant it to. With such a solitary life, Phoebe often felt that she was losing the habit of knowing how to talk to people.

"Um, I'd like a book about King Arthur. If that's okay with you. And his knights. The ones of the Round Table."

"I'm pretty sure those are the only ones he had."

"I can probably find what I want by myself if you'll

just tell me where to look. I don't want to inconvenience you if you'd like to join the celebration."

"No," Phoebe said, a trifle too strongly. She moderated her voice. "No. I'm happy about the little princess, of course." She didn't want him to think she wasn't. "But my duties are here."

"That's very . . ." He paused. "Punctilious."

Punctilious? Is he making these words up? As usual when Phoebe didn't know what to say, she spouted one of the odd facts that she had gleaned from her long days reading in the library.

"Did you know that a hogshead is a wooden cask holding sixty-three gallons? It's bigger than an ordinary barrel, you know."

"Yes," the young man said. "I do know. I work in the blacksmith shop. We make the iron bands that hold them together. For the cooper."

"Oh." This was the first time anyone had responded to one of her odd facts with anything but a puzzled stare. Once again she didn't know what to say. Just as she was about to give him another fact, she remembered what he wanted. "Oh. Your book."

Phoebe went to the stacks and ran her finger across

the spines of several volumes until she found the one she wanted and plucked it off the shelf. "I like this one especially well," she said. "The drawings are very nice." She knew the purpose of a library was to lend books, but it was hard for her to let go of them.

Gently he took the book from her hands. "I've had one book about King Arthur since I was little and it's still in perfect condition. I'll take very good care of this one, I promise."

It was as if he knew what she was thinking. Reluctantly she opened the ledger where she kept track of the checked-out books, all the while keeping an eye on how carefully he was holding his. "What's your name?"

"My name? Why do you need my name?" He hugged the book to his chest.

"It's the rules. I need to know who has that book. Rules are important, don't you think?" She dipped her quill into the ink pot and waited.

"Yes, of course they are. But could I just tell you where I live?"

"I'll need that, too. In case I have to come retrieve my book. I mean *the* book."

"You won't. I promise."

She shook her head and waited. The silence length-ened.

Finally he took a deep breath and said, "Sebastian."

"Have we met before?"

He swallowed. "I doubt it. I don't go out much. And Maurice, the main blacksmith, handles all the business of dealing with the public. I just make things."

"Okay. But I need more than just a first name. Who is your family?"

He made a small sound in his throat. Then he took a deep breath, exhaled, and said wearily, "My family? I don't have much family, but everyone knows of my father. He's Vlad." And then he squared his shoulders and raised his voice. "Yes, that's right, Vlad. The exiled poisoner-in-chief under Queen Olympia. The creator of the Dragon's Sweat poison."

"The creator of the Take Seven Steps and Die poison, too?" Phoebe asked carefully.

Sebastian nodded. "The very one. Can I still have the book?"

How could she, the daughter of the exiled torturer-in-chief, say no to him, even though she was now afraid, and very, very sorry she'd been unpleasant? She knew *she* was nothing like her own feared and hated father, even if no one else seemed to believe that. Who was she to judge?

Nobody, but it was pretty hard not to. Even for her.

She cleared her throat. "Of course," she said, ducking her head so he couldn't see her flushed cheeks. As she made an entry in her ledger, her hand shook and she made a blot over his name. Not that she was likely to forget it.

"How long can I keep it?" he asked.

She was tempted to say *forever*, just so he'd never come back. But she had a librarian's duty to treat every patron the same, and to safeguard the books. "Three weeks. But you can renew it for another three weeks if you haven't finished."

"Three weeks should be sufficient," he said, then turned and left, closing the door behind him.

Phoebe put down the quill and pressed her shaking fingers to her cheeks. Sebastian had seemed familiar because Vlad and her father, Boris, had been close friends, had collaborated on various horrible projects, had consulted with each other on their individual grue-some enterprises. Certainly she had heard Sebastian's name before. They might even have played together as children.

But why wasn't Sebastian in exile with Vlad? Why was he tucked away in the blacksmith shop? Had he and Phoebe both been spared from exile because they had never done anything wrong, in spite of their fa-thers' efforts to have them follow in their rotten pa-ternal footsteps? She herself had been judged mature enough to decide if she wanted to accompany her ex-iled father, out of loyalty, or to remain in the kingdom. She hadn't needed a second to think about it. Living in virtual hiding was vastly preferable to spending another day with the father who had always frightened and re-pelled her. Perhaps Sebastian had been given the same choice.

If that was true, she should have been much nicer to him. Oh, why didn't she think more before she acted?

She turned to the window, through which came the sounds of singing and laughing and clapping to music, and knew that even if she were out there in the crowds, there would be an empty space all around her. And the same was doubtless true for Sebastian.

Oh, dear. She definitely should have been nicer to him.

2

QUEEN MARIGOLD, KING CHRISTIAN, and former King Swithbert—the queen's father and now royal grandfather—sat in rocking chairs in the nursery, passing a sleeping baby Poppy from one to the other like a football. They all wanted to hold her, but didn't want to appear too greedy or selfish about her.

The little rag-mop dogs, Flopsy, Mopsy, and Topsy, kept trying to get into Marigold's lap. They had always done so, before this squalling red creature had shown up, but were now being told—over and *over*—that they had to lie on their floor pillows. They were not taking this news gracefully. There had been a few accidents that the castle chambermaids had had to clean up, and Marigold's favorite pair of slippers had been mysteriously chewed to pieces.

Big, shaggy Bub had gotten the message the first time he had stuck his giant muzzle into the cradle and been shooed away by Christian. Christian, whom he had loved and protected throughout his entire life! Bub was now spending most of his time forlornly under a bed in a far bedroom. Spoiled, petite Cate, whose fanciest tricks and most dramatic hysterics had been almost completely ignored, was there with him, pouting and seething while he moped.

"Does she look like I did when I was a baby, Papa?" Marigold asked, brushing Flopsy's paws off her skirt. Flopsy went off to chew up a stuffed lamb that Poppy had kicked out of her cradle onto the floor.

"I believe she does," Swithbert said, prolonging his turn at holding Poppy by pretending to scrutinize her features. "And every bit as pretty and smart, too."

Marigold laughed. "How can you tell she's smart?" she asked, even though she was positive he was correct, since Poppy was obviously the best baby to ever have been born. She just wanted him to keep going on about this exceptional child.

"I can tell by the way her eyebrows are twitching, even in her sleep," Swithbert said. "Mrs. Clover says that's a sure sign of intelligence in babies. And very rare."

Mrs. Clover was the head housekeeper of Zandelphia-Beaurivage castle, and the object of a romantic tug of war between Swithbert and Wendell, the retired wizard who now lived at the castle along with his huge white elephant, Hannibal, with which Marigold was endlessly fascinated. Swithbert worried that Wendell had the upper hand with Mrs. Clover, mainly because of his fabulous elephant, but also because Swithbert himself was nothing but a has-been king now that he had retired so Christian and Marigold could rule.

King Christian tried to keep from grinning extravagantly as Swithbert finally handed Poppy to him, but he couldn't help himself. The little princess was such an unfathomable miracle, such a promise to the future, such a fascination, that she seemed almost as if she were a mythical creature.

"When do you think you'll be having the Welcome Party?" Swithbert asked his daughter.

A cloud passed over Marigold's face and she cast an anxious glance at Poppy. It was at Marigold's own Welcome Party that she had been bestowed by an overzealous (or perhaps careless) fairy with the very *un*welcome gift of being able to read people's thoughts. Marigold had overcome it by now, but she never wanted such a thing to happen to Poppy.

"Do you think it would be rude, Papa, if I asked the fairies not to bring gifts?"

"I'm afraid it would be, precious. It's traditional, you know, for them to give something special to each new royal baby."

Marigold frowned. "Maybe I could have Wendell check out each gift before it's actually given away. He's still enough of a wizard to do that, isn't he?"

Swithbert hated to consider that Wendell could do things that he himself could not—especially if Mrs. Clover was watching—but he had to be fair. Reluctantly he said, "He very well could be. You should ask him."

"I will. Now I'm going to tell you one more elephant joke and then it'll be my turn for Poppy."

Inwardly Christian groaned. He hated Marigold's elephant jokes almost as much as he had hated her previous obsession, the very confusing knock-knock jokes.

"What time is it when ten elephants are chasing you?" Marigold asked.

"I don't know," Chris said. "Too late?"

"No, silly." She giggled in advance of her punch line. "It's ten after one. Get it? Ten after one?"

Chris sighed.

"Now hand her over."

Phoebe opened the library's leaded-glass window just enough to let in a solid wedge of cold air, and to hear the evening crier out in the square yelling the latest news. (There had been a recent eruption of smoke and flames from the dragon, who had been rather quiet for most of the winter; Maeve the unicorn had had twins, one pink and one blue; on Market Day the stalls doing the biggest business were those selling the little striped squashes, the detail-perfect miniatures, the glass-bead necklaces, and the least stinky cheeses, though the crier himself preferred the ones that smelled like old

socks. Not everyone's taste, he knew, but anyway . . .
Extra firewood could be picked up outside the cooper's
workshop.)

Winter was on the way out. Soon darkness would
fall later, there would be no ice in the morning wash-
basin, and there would be even fewer visitors at the
library. Phoebe thought summer was always the perfect time to sit out in the sunny gardens, reading, but
the problem seemed to be that people stayed out in
the gardens doing something else—weeding? games?
courtship?—and didn't want to tear themselves away
long enough to come into the quiet, orderly library.
Even Queen Marigold and King Christian, normally
big readers, were reading less since Princess Poppy
had shown up. The servants who usually came in to
borrow books for the royal family hadn't been by for
weeks.

Phoebe shut the window and burrowed into her
shawl. She should be closing up and going home, but
she liked the library better than the dank stone quarters that had been Boris's. She'd had nowhere else to
live after her father's exile, so she had scrubbed and
painted and brought in colorful fabrics and pillows. But

certain nasty stains proved impossible to remove, and she remembered all too well the torture devices that had once stood where she now had her little kitchen table and her wardrobe, and her rocker and footstool.

Boris's instruments of torture had been ordered to be destroyed when he was sent away, but Phoebe was pretty sure he had managed to take his favorites with him—the Tongue Tearer, the Roman Pincers, the White-Hot Mitt, and the Dragon's Teeth. Boris especially loved the Dragon's Teeth. He had invented it because he loved dragons—their size, their ability to throw flames, their armor-plated scales. All of it fascinated him. It was a passion he shared with Vlad, but Vlad, who was of a different sensibility than Boris was, loved dragons for their cleverness, their wiliness, their beautiful iridescence. And he, too, had an invention that honored the dragon: the infamous and dreaded Dragon's Sweat poison.

Phoebe imagined Vlad had smuggled some of it, as well as other toxic mixtures, into exile with him, just as Boris had done with some of his own tools of the trade. It had been a happy day when evil Queen Olympia had fallen into the river, after which King Swithbert had put a stop to all the poisoning and torturing that Olympia had encouraged, and then exiled the perpetrators. Phoebe knew she could never forgive her father for all the terrible cruelties he had inflicted—the damage he had done to her own life was nothing compared to that—and she also knew she never wanted to see him again.

As she put away the books she had been reading, she realized it had been almost three weeks since Sebastian had borrowed the King Arthur book. She hoped he would bring it back on his own, because she didn't want to have to track him down to retrieve it; he might be living in Vlad's previous quarters. They were certain to be nicer than her own inherited rooms (Vlad loved fine things, while Boris could care less), yet she didn't want to set foot in a place where poisonous vapors had once floated.

She trudged homeward, thinking, *Maybe he'll return it tomorrow.*

After a consultation, the wizard Wendell had said he believed he *could* determine if any of the fairy gifts were dangerous—on purpose or inadvertently—and Marigold hoped this was true.

She wished she didn't have to have the Welcome Party at all. She wanted only to be with Christian and Poppy, in their private quarters, reading and talking, telling elephant jokes and playing together. She must remember to include the dogs, too. She knew Flopsy, Mopsy and Topsy were unhappy about being relegated to their floor pillows and, come to think about it, she hadn't even seen Bub and Cate in a long time. Oh, it was wicked of her to have neglected them so. But having Poppy had preoccupied and distracted her, and she knew she wasn't paying as much attention to a lot of other things as she was to Poppy, even though there was a nursemaid to help with the baby.

Marigold liked the nursemaid, a comfortably upholstered lady named Mrs. Sunday, but she would have preferred to have only herself and Christian caring for Poppy. It was unreasonable for a queen to think that way, she supposed, but that's just how it was. There was another new servant just to do the baby's washing—who knew such a little person could produce such heaps of laundry?—and still *another* new servant to keep track of the baby presents pouring in from all over the known world, and to draft thank-you notes.

Marigold couldn't possibly write all the notes herself, but she did want to see them, just to make sure they were properly appreciative and respectful, and to personally sign them before they were p-mailed.

The queen was having more trouble than she'd anticipated getting her routine in order.

3

THE FINAL COLD RAIN of winter—or maybe the first one of spring—flung itself against the library windows, as if it were angry at not being allowed in where the fire hissed and crackled in the chimney corner and candlelight glossed the warm colors of the book bindings.

Phoebe ignored the rain as she concentrated on the book she was reading. It was full of interesting facts, ones she'd probably never get to tell anybody else, but she liked to think that she was nevertheless keeping her mind well-furnished. Wasn't it nice to know that robins could live twelve years, and that your fingernails could grow two inches in one year, and that most rats were right-handed?

She closed the book. Who but she would ever care about such things?

She jumped when the door opened and Sebastian came in, shaking off his umbrella and propping it by the door.

"I brought back the King Arthur book." His tone suggested she might not have expected him to.

"That . . . that's good. Do you want to renew it?"

"No. I got what I nee—"

Just then there was a terrific *thud*. Sebastian had been facing the window. "I think that was a p-mail pigeon! The storm must have blown him into the glass." He turned and ran for the door.

"Where are you going?"

"Out to get him! There's a shortage of them already, you know. We can't afford to lose one. And he may be carrying an important message. Get a towel ready for him!" And he dashed out, forgetting his umbrella.

A towel? Where did he think she would find a towel in a library? And who did he think he was, ordering her around like that? And what did a poisoner's son care about a battered pigeon, anyway?

While Phoebe was thinking all these thoughts, she

was nevertheless scurrying around looking for something like a towel. She settled for one of the cloths she used to dust the books, which she found just as Sebastian came racing back, soaking wet and shivering, with a limp pigeon in his hands.

My turn to give orders, Phoebe thought. "Get over there by the fire," she commanded. "And wrap him in this." She handed Sebastian the dust cloth. "And here. This is for you." She flung her shawl across his dripping shoulders—big broad ones, she couldn't help noticing. "Is it alive?"

"I think so." He wrapped the cloth around the bird and set it on the hearth, rubbing it gently. "But look. The cylinder's broken open."

"Well, read the message," Phoebe said. "It's got to be important. Who would send a p-mail in this kind of weather if it wasn't? And this pigeon's not going to be delivering any messages in his condition. You may have to do it."

"You keep massaging the pigeon, then," Sebastian said.

Phoebe took the bird in her hands and felt the fast

beat of its tiny heart under her fingers. "Come on, birdie," she whispered. "Don't give up."

Sebastian worked at unrolling the wet paper. "The ink is running, but I think I can make it out." He spread the strip of paper on the hearth and read:

M. Do not wait. Take the baby instantly.
Leave the ransom note.
We will wait in the agreed-upon place.
B. and V.

"Whoa!" he said, sitting back on his heels. "Look at this. What do you think it means?"

Phoebe bent over the note, the pigeon still in her hands, and read the blurry words out loud. "Oh, my," she said. "Is that what you read, too?"

"Yes." He paused. "Which is the only baby in the kingdom worth kidnapping?"

"Princess Poppy, you mean?"

"Can you think of another one worth a ransom?"

"But who's M.? And who are B. and V.?" She felt a terrible sense of dread.

"I don't know who M. is, but I'm pretty sure who B. and V. are. I told you who my father is, and he's probably part of this. He wants revenge. He was pretty outraged that he was exiled."

After a long pause, Phoebe said quietly, "So was mine."

Sebastian gave her a close look. "Why would *your* father be outraged about *my* father's exile?"

"He wasn't outraged about your father," she said, unsure why she was telling him this. "He was outraged about himself." The pigeon began to stir in her hands.

"You mean . . . you mean, your father is Boris? As in 'B.'?"

She nodded, trying to soothe the pigeon, who was struggling to work his way out of the cloth wrapped around him.

"Your father is Boris, the torturer-in-chief?" Sebastian sounded unbelieving.

"Yes, yes," she affirmed. "Do you want to make something of that?" Maybe telling him had been a mistake. She unwrapped the pigeon, who was beginning to move his wings.

"No. Not at all. I'm just . . . surprised. I knew he had a daughter. We may even have played together a few times when we were little. But I never knew what happened to you."

"I've kept a low profile. Like you have. My father wasn't the most popular person in the kingdom, you know. And the library was perfect for me. I love to read and I needed a job where nobody would have to work with me. People are scared of me."

"I do know. I know all about that. Even if you've never done anything to make anybody fear you, they still do. Just because of what someone else has done."

They studied each other, forgetting all about the pigeon, who was rapidly regaining his strength and fluttering his wings.

"You *do* know," Phoebe murmured, almost to herself.

With a great flapping, the pigeon rose into the air and flew around the library, the open message cylinder hanging from his leg.

"Oh, no!" Sebastian yelled, reaching toward the fire and then yanking his hand back.

"What?"

"When the pigeon took off, his wings blew the p-mail message into the fire."

"But isn't that a good thing?" Phoebe asked. "Now M., whoever that is, won't get the message and so won't kidnap the baby."

"Maybe not *tonight*," Sebastian told her. "But do you think that will stop B. and V.? We need to report this, but now we have no proof to take to the captain of the guards."

"We can just tell him. Can't we?"

"Even if we could get in to see him—which is doubtful, considering who we are—why would he believe us without any evidence? We don't have much credibility, thanks to our fathers."

"But a threat against Princess Poppy—he'd be crazy to ignore that."

"Then, I suppose we have to try." Sebastian shivered and handed her back her shawl. "And we should do it right now. There's no time to waste."

Phoebe flung the damp shawl over her shoulders, grabbed her own umbrella, and left with Sebastian, locking the library door behind her and leaving the pigeon flapping around the high ceiling. She hoped there wouldn't be too much cleaning up after him to do when she got back, and then felt petty for worrying about that when the princess's life was at stake. But practicalities have to be tended to, even during emergencies.

They rushed through the downpour, across the deserted town square, to the guard quarters, then stood for a moment outside the heavy closed door. They looked at each other, nodded, and then Sebastian raised the big iron knocker and pounded.

A beefy guard with a tankard in his hand and the top button of his uniform undone opened the door and peered out. "What is it?" he demanded.

"We have a possible kidnapping to report," Sebastian told him.

"A kidnapping? Don't tell me. You suspect somebody wants to grab Princess Poppy. Right?"

"Yes! Right!" Sebastian exclaimed. "How did you know?"

"Because we've been getting at least one report like that every day since she was born. Seems like everybody in the kingdom thinks there's kidnapping plans afoot. Usually to be committed by a neighbor they've recently had an argument with."

"But this one is—" Sebastian began.

The guard opened the door wider. "Come on in. I'll let you fill out a form, just like everybody else." They stepped inside, politely leaving their dripping umbrellas propped inside the door. "Of course, we'll need your evidence."

"We had some," Phoebe said. "But it burned up."

"Funny how often that seems to happen once people have a form to fill out." The guard pointed them to a table and sailed a form at them. "There's quills and ink on the table. Go to it."

"Is the captain around?" Sebastian asked. "I think he should hear this."

"Yeah, Rollo's here. But he hates to be interrupted when he's eating. Who should I say wants to see him?"

"My name's Phoebe. I work in the library." Librarians were supposed to be respectable and harmless, weren't they? And who would remember that Boris, the torturer-in-chief, had a daughter named Phoebe? He'd been gone for more than two years.

"And I'm Sebastian."

"You're kidding me, aren't you?" the guard said. "You're not really the kids of Boris, the torturer-in-chief, and Vlad, the poisoner-in-chief. This is some kind of joke, right? Or a scheme to distract us, get us working on some fake crime while you're off committing something else?"

"Of course not," Phoebe said indignantly. "Why would we do that?"

"Oh, I don't know," the guard said, rolling his eyes. "Because your fathers were the two nastiest, scariest, most devious brutes this kingdom has ever seen, and were more than capable of cooking up some elaborate ruse so suspicion would never fall on them. The nuts don't fall far from the tree, as my pal Edric would say."

"Do you mean you don't believe us? That you're not going to let us talk to Rollo?"

"Get out of here," the guard growled. "Your 'report'"—he made quotation mark signs with his fingers—"is one I can be certain is a fake. And I sure don't have to bother Rollo with your fairy tale."

"But—" Sebastian began.

"Get out! Before I lock the two of you up for false—well, false *something*. Go!" He put down his tankard, grabbed each of them by an arm, and hustled them to the door. "And don't come back." He flung them into the rain, without their umbrellas, and slammed the door behind them.

"I told you," Sebastian said.

"That's helpful," Phoebe said, crossing her arms and turning her back on him.

"Well, what *would* be helpful? And what do we do now? We've got a credible threat that no one will believe, no evidence of it, and a princess in jeopardy. We can't do nothing."

"We also can't stand here arguing about it. We're getting soaked and cold, and that pigeon is probably pooping all over my books. Let's talk about this in front of a fire."

They hurried back across the square to the library, where, yes, the pigeon had left his mark on a significant percentage of the library. *At least he seems to be fully recovered from his smash into the library window*, Phoebe thought as she mopped up the droppings. Unfortunately, it was still raining too hard to open that same window and toss him out.

Sebastian stood in front of the fire, dripping. "There's only one thing to do," he said. "We have to go to the king and queen."

"Oh, right," Phoebe said. "We couldn't get even one slovenly guard to pay any attention to us, never mind Rollo. How do you think we can get in to see the king and queen?"

"Aren't we supposed to be the descendants of the two wiliest, cleverest brutes this kingdom has ever seen? Surely we can think of something."

"*You* think. I've got a lot of cleaning up to do."

"I need to get into some dry clothes. I'm freezing. And you must be, too."

She was, but she didn't want to admit it. "Well, keep thinking while you go change. Because I can't figure out any way to solve this, no matter how clever a brute I'm related to."

Sebastian stopped at the door, his hand on the knob. "I don't care how clever and wily my father was. He was also just like that guard said—nasty and scary, too.

And I hope with everything I can hope with that there's not one bit of him in me. I'm going to have to be clever and imaginative on my own."

He went out and shut the door very quietly. It was as effective as if he'd slammed it.

Phoebe stood, the cleanup cloth in her hand. What he'd said was so exactly what she thought about Boris, her torturer-in-chief father, that she felt like crying. She wished she'd been able to tell Sebastian one of her odd facts in gratitude. Maybe how most people's ears don't match.

The pigeon finally got tired of circling the library and settled on a stack of folios, tucked his head under his wing, and went to sleep.

Phoebe wrapped her spare shawl around her wet shoulders, plopped down in her chair, put her chin in her hand, and tried to do some clever and imaginative thinking herself while she listened to the evening crier.

"Princess Poppy has learned to roll over and may be cutting her first tooth!Abnormally early, I know, but we didn't expect our little princess to be an ordinary baby, did we? Of course not! And she is not! Her Welcome Party is scheduled for five weeks hence! Invitations were sent by p-mail today!" He coughed. Being a crier, especially in bad weather, required a certain vocal stamina not everyone had. "More news at ten! Learn who was caught stealing apples from the castle storeroom! Hear how many trees the dragon ignited today!" He coughed again. "And if you haven't already noticed, it's windy and pouring rain, even though it's supposed to be spring!"

4

As much as Marigold didn't want to start being queen again, she knew she had to. That was one of the problems with being a responsible regent—sometimes it was nothing but a big drag. What she wanted to do was hang around the nursery, elbowing Mrs. Sunday out of the way. She loved it when the laundress came in with a pile of Poppy's little clothes. She couldn't help herself—she just had to *oooh* over how adorable they were. And she hated it when the secretary came in with a pile of thank-you notes to go over. She couldn't do that in a hurry. After all, she really was very grateful for the outpouring of love and generosity from her subjects (even though there might have been an element of self-interest involved; someday when they needed a favor from the queen, they could remind her of the cunning little blanket they had knit with their very own arthritic hands) and wanted to be properly appreciative.

And before you knew it, Mrs. Sunday was the one holding Poppy and fussing over her, and Marigold was back to being more queen than mommy.

"Go on now, Your Highness." Mrs. Sunday smiled at Poppy, who giggled back at her, making Marigold want to snatch the baby away—and to push poor innocent Mrs. Sunday out the window. She knew it was good for Poppy to be loved by many people and to love many people, too. But Marigold could hardly stand it.

"We've got everything under control here," Mrs. Sunday said. "You *are* the queen. You must have important things you need to do."

She certainly did. There was no question that she'd neglected her queenly duties for weeks now. Even Christian, as devoted a father as anyone could be, had realized that he had obligations and so had resumed his usual routine as king, modified to include time to play with his daughter.

Disconsolately, Marigold made her way through the labyrinth of hallways toward the throne room. As she went, she realized she hadn't heard enough really good new elephant jokes to satisfy her since Poppy was born. And she'd been shamefully thoughtless and inconsiderate with the dogs. And she had no idea what was happening with her perfume business. She hadn't even worn her crown for weeks, an unseemly thing for a monarch to do.

She was so busy thinking, she almost bumped into two people coming toward her. "Oh, sorry."

"Maybe you can help us," Phoebe said, then gave Marigold a close look. "Has anybody ever told you that you look a lot like the queen?"

"I get that all the time," Marigold said, embarrassed to be caught without her crown. "What do you need?"

"It's important that we talk to King Christian or Queen Marigold," Phoebe told her. "The sentries told us that they're unavailable and said we should leave. But we remembered they made a promise at their coronation to always be attentive to the needs of their subjects. So we . . . well, we kind of sneaked in when the sentries were distracted."

"Yes, they did say that," Marigold said, her guilt at her royal neglect growing.

"We have something very important to tell them. It's a matter of life or death," Sebastian said.

"Oh, my!" Marigold was alarmed. She needed Chris with her for this. "Why don't you come with me and we'll see if we can get this straightened out."

She led them up some stairs and down a few more corridors before arriving at the throne room. Two uniformed guards holding pikes stood at the door. When they saw her, they bowed and murmured, "Your Highness."

Phoebe and Sebastian stopped dead. "Your Highness?" Sebastian said. "You mean you really are—"

"Yes," Marigold said, embarrassed. "I know I should have introduced myself, but I wasn't wearing my crown and I've become a little rusty at being the queen, so I—well, anyway, come on in." She gestured to the guards and they opened the doors to the throne room.

Chris was playing Snipsnapsnorum at a table with the wizard Wendell, ex-king Swithbert, the troll Edric, and Magnus, the court architect. They all looked up, their eyebrows raised with curiosity.

"Hi, Papa. Wendell. Ed. Magnus. Chris. This is—oh, I forgot to get your names, though you both do look familiar. Anyway, they say they have something to tell us. Something of life-and-death importance."

Chris stood up and dropped his cards on the table. "What is it?"

He always seemed to know, Marigold thought with affection, which things to take seriously and which not to. Probably the word *death* had done it, she considered.

"Your Highness, thank you for seeing us," Sebastian said. "We apologize for not making an appointment, but this couldn't wait." He lowered his voice. "Is it okay to talk in front of them?" he asked, indicating the other card players.

"Yes, of course. But if you'd prefer, we could go into my private chambers."

Phoebe and Sebastian looked at each other and nodded. Neither wished to have their identities revealed to any more people than absolutely necessary now that they had managed to create a little anonymity for themselves.

"Keep playing," Christian said to Swithbert, Ed, Wendell, and Magnus. "I know my presence has never discouraged any of you from cheating."

"You got that right," Swithbert said.

"Not me," Magnus said. "I only cheat when I have to. When everybody else does."

"Somehow even magic isn't enough help in Snip-snapsnorum," Wendell said. "Cheating becomes *necessary.*"

"You do the same when the circumstances are on the other foot, Chris," Ed said. (It had taken a while, but eventually the court residents had gotten used to Ed's creative expressions. Sometimes they even knew what he was talking about.)

"I'm afraid you're right," Chris said. He and Marigold walked with Phoebe and Sebastian to a tall door with an ornate iron closure. This door opened into a large, comfortably furnished sitting room. A fire blazed in the hearth, and the heavy velvet drapes were open to the wet and fading daylight. Chris gestured to a big plush sofa, and Phoebe and Sebastian sat—on the edge, their hands on their knees, as if prepared to leap up and run if they had to. Christian and Marigold sat across from them in two high-backed chairs.

"Now," Chris said, "what's this life-and-death thing?"

Phoebe looked at Sebastian. Sebastian looked at Phoebe. He took a deep breath, then said, "Somebody's going to kidnap Princess Poppy."

Marigold gasped so loudly, Chris reached over to pat her on the back, as if she were choking. She put her hand to her mouth and said, "Who? When? I was just in the nursery and everything was fine. What makes you think this could happen?"

Sebastian told them about the pigeon and the intercepted message—and what it was about and what had happened to it. "So we have no proof, and we don't know who the message was intended for. But we believe it."

"And why is that?" Chris asked.

They were silent.

As the silence stretched on, Chris continued. "Do you have any idea how many threats we receive every week? As peaceful as the kingdom of Zandelphia-Beaurivage is now, there are days when I think everybody in it is annoyed about something and they want to take it out on me. So I need to know why you think this one is serious."

Finally Phoebe spoke. "Because we're sure we know who sent the message, and we know what they're capable of."

"And how do you know this?"

Sometimes Marigold was in awe of just how kingly Chris could be. The forceful way he now spoke to the two on the couch made it inconceivable that they could refuse to answer. Yet, for a moment, it seemed that they were going to.

Finally the girl spoke again. "Because one of them is my father. Boris, the ex-torturer-in-chief."

"And the other," the young man said softly, "is Vlad, the ex-poisoner-in-chief. *My* father."

Marigold gasped again, but more quietly this time. "I *knew* you looked familiar," she said.

Chris patted the queen's hand absent-mindedly. "Yes. You're Phoebe, and you're Sebastian," he said.

"You knew?" Sebastian asked.

Christian nodded. "I'm the king. It's my business to know."

"But," Phoebe went on, "we're nothing like our fathers. At least I'm not. I don't know him very well"—she gestured at Sebastian—"so I can't be sure, but I think he's okay. And I do know our fathers were close friends and that this is exactly something they would do. Boris was so outraged about his exile that he vowed revenge. He said it was best served cold, whatever that means."

"It means that you can make a better plan for vengeance and carry it out more effectively when your anger has cooled off and you're icy and merciless," Sebastian said.

The word *merciless* was so accurate and so chilling that Phoebe shivered. "Oh. Then that's what he meant. And it sounds awful, doesn't it?"

"It does to me," Marigold said. She turned to Chris. "Do you mean there have been other threats against Poppy? And you didn't tell me?"

He put his hand over hers. "I didn't want to worry you, my love. Rollo and I had it under control. Why spoil your happiness with Poppy?"

She yanked her hand away. "I thought we were best friends! I thought you told me everything! How dare you keep something like that from me? Have you forgotten I'm also the *queen*? You don't need to *protect* me. I'm perfectly capable of deciding for myself how much something worries me. And I can't do that unless I know what the problem *is*. It's insulting, that's what it is." Furious tears welled in her eyes.

Since he'd married Marigold, Chris had learned a thing or two about what *happily ever after* really meant. He was smart enough to recognize that he'd just screwed up and that a real apology (not one of those that somehow suggests that another person is actually at fault because they couldn't take a joke or were too sensitive, or something like that) was called for. Immediately.

"I'm sorry, precious," he said. "I thought I was saving you from worry, but I see that I was wrong. Can you forgive me?" A good apologizer offers the offended party an opportunity to be generous in forgiveness—but doesn't count on it. Some people (luckily Marigold was not one of them) can hold a grudge forever.

"Probably," Marigold said. "In fact, I'm sure I can. But first I want to hear what else Phoebe and Sebastian have to say."

"Oh," Phoebe said. "Nothing, really. We told you all of it."

"So you don't know who M. is, or where the pigeon was headed?" Chris asked.

"No," Sebastian said. "But I'd guess it was going to your personal quarters. Anybody who could get close enough to Princess Poppy to snatch her would have to be someone who knew how to get to her. Someone who knew the castle well. Don't you think?"

"Indeed I do," Christian said. "Don't you, precious?" he asked Marigold, who nodded. "So the first thing we're going to do is increase the security in the nursery."

"And you should probably find everyone in the castle whose name begins with *M* and start investigating them," Sebastian said. Then, realizing how presumptuous he'd been, he stammered, "Except the queen, of course." He bowed in Marigold's direction. "Don't you think? Your Highness?"

"You make perfect sense," Christian said, then looked at Marigold. "What do you think, precious?"

"That's exactly what we're going to do," Marigold said. "Immediately."

Christian stood up. "Mrs. Clover will have a list of everybody who works in the castle. I'll have someone fetch it while we get over to the nursery. And we must tell the others."

When they opened the door to the throne room, the card players looked up.

"Poppy may be in danger," Marigold said. "We're on the way to the nursery to check on her."

"Then we're coming, too," Swithbert said, throwing down his cards.

As they made their way through the corridors, Chris said, "There must be fifty people here whose first or last names start with *M*, beginning with Meg, the kitchen maid who's married to Rollo. I can just imagine how he'd take to the suggestion that his wife might be planning a major crime."

Phoebe and Sebastian exchanged a glance as each of them thought, *Thank goodness we never got to talk to Rollo.*

"We have three new staff members with access to

the nursery," Marigold said, alarmed. "Mrs. Sunday, the laundress, and the secretary. I don't know if any of their names start with M. We need to have the crier announce this threat. The whole kingdom has to be on the lookout for any strange behavior. We cannot let this happen."

Christian was thinking about how much strange behavior seemed to go on in the kingdom even on the most unremarkable day. For one thing, there was a great white elephant parked in the stables next to the unicorns, who had never really gotten used to him and tried to stampede away whenever he raised his trunk and trumpeted, ramming into whatever got in their way. The stalls were pierced with unicorn-horn holes.

There was also a wizard who would cheat at cards with a retired king, a current king, the kingdom's architect, and a troll. And Christian himself had once been a servant in this very castle. Zandelphia-Beaurivage wasn't exactly an ordinary kingdom.

Chris put his arms around Marigold and said, "Perhaps, my love, we need a little more information before we tip our hand. Don't you think that for now it's better that the culprits don't know we're on to them? They may not be as careful if they think their plot is still a secret."

Something flipped inside Phoebe's chest when she saw how tender the king was with the queen, even right on the heels of an argument. She must have made a little sound as she thought about this, because Sebastian said quietly, "What? Do you dispute?"

"Huh? Dispute? No. I mean, I don't know. He's the king. He knows better than me. Doesn't he?"

"But we know our fathers." Sebastian coughed to get the king's attention. "Excuse me, sire," he said. "I know Vlad—and Boris, too, though not as well—and I haven't forgotten that they're clever and ruthless and impatient. Once they get an idea, they'll want to get it done."

"But we intercepted the message," Phoebe said. "M. doesn't know anything about the plan."

Sebastian turned to face her. "Do you think they would have sent that pigeon out into the storm if they weren't in a hurry? What makes you think they sent only one pigeon? Wouldn't your father make sure there was a backup, just in case the first one didn't get through? I know mine would."

"And so would mine," Phoebe agreed miserably.

Without a word, Marigold picked up her pace, and the others followed.

The crowd burst into the yellow and purple nursery expecting to find a surprised Mrs. Sunday and a sleeping infant.

They found an empty room.

No Mrs. Sunday.

No baby in the cradle.

Nothing.

5

Marigold was on the verge of a scream when she heard muffled sounds coming from behind the curtained doorway that led to Mrs. Sunday's sleeping quarters. She pulled back the curtain and saw Mrs. Sunday lying on the bed. Marigold was about to fire her on the spot for neglecting her little charge and taking a nap when she noticed that Mrs. Sunday had no choice about being neglectful: she was bound hand and foot, and gagged.

Magnus, quiet and competent as always, began untying her and pulling the gag from her mouth, while Ed, excitable as always, yelled, "What happened? What happened? Who did this? Who did this?" The rest stood in shock.

Mrs. Sunday sat up and burst into tears. "Oh, Your Highness," she wailed, her hands over her face. "I tried to stop them, but I wasn't strong enough."

"Who?" Marigold demanded. "Who was it? And where is Poppy?"

"They took her." Mrs. Sunday let out another heartbroken wail. "She's gone."

Christian sat on the edge of the bed and took Mrs. Sunday's hands in his. "Mrs. Sunday," he said severely. "If you tell me you had nothing to do with this, I will believe you. But then you must tell me everything you know about what happened."

Mrs. Sunday took a deep breath and said, "I had nothing to do with it, I swear. The first I knew that anything was wrong was when the laundress came in the nursery with her laundry basket. I thought it was rather late for her to be bringing laundry. I was just putting Poppy to bed. And she had two footmen with her, which was odd. One of them, Fogarty, was hired for banquet services, I was told, so I wondered what he was doing here. The other one I've seen here and there.

A general errand boy, I think. He's young and seems a little befuddled. I believe his name is Bartholomew.

"The two footmen grabbed me and slapped a gag on me before I could scream or say anything, and then they dragged me in here and tied me up. I could see that laundress put Poppy in the basket and cover her with a sheet. She put something in the cradle, too. Then they pulled the curtain so I couldn't see anything else, but I heard the door close and then I didn't hear anything more. The storm was noisy, so I might have missed something." She removed her hands from Chris's grasp and started wailing again.

"Thank you, Mrs. Sunday," Chris said calmly, as if his child were not in unknown peril. "One more thing. Do you know what the laundress's name is?"

"It's Emlyn, sire. Though mostly we just called her Laundress."

"Emlyn," Chris said. "Em. Or letter *M.*"

"They can't have been gone long," Marigold said, suddenly businesslike. "They may even still be in the castle. I'll alert Rollo." She ran from the room.

"Swithbert," Chris addressed his father-in-law. "How many ways are there out of the castle?"

"Oh, my," Swithbert said, still in shock. "I don't know that I ever counted them." He held up his fingers and started ticking them off as he mentally calculated. This went on for quite a while. Finally, he said, "There are thirty-seven that I can think of just offhand. Probably more."

"Don't forget the secret passage down in the dungeon," Magnus said.

"Right," said Chris. "That's at least thirty-eight."

"Well, what are we waiting for?" Ed exclaimed. "We've got to get down to brass roots and find Poppy!"

But first they looked at what was left in the cradle, which was indeed a ransom note, demanding a very large number of ducats—and signed by B. and V., the Terrible Twos.

Rollo rallied his guards (except for the one who hadn't told him of the attempted report of a kidnapping; he was now assigned to elephant-poop-shoveling duties in the stables). He sent them to all the castle exits anybody could think of, but by the early morning, no one had passed through them who shouldn't have, and definitely nobody with a laundry basket. Rollo sure didn't want to give that news to the king and queen, who were already pretty upset that he hadn't seen Phoebe and Sebastian when they first came to make a report. He was glad he had the poop-shoveling guard to blame, though, secretly, he was pretty sure he, too, would have refused to give an audience to the progeny of the worst brutes the kingdom had ever seen.

Since King Christian and Queen Marigold had assumed reign over Zandelphia-Beaurivage, everyone in the kingdom who had ever been fans of ex-queen Olympia and the Terrible Twos was busily forgetting that fact, and hoping that anyone else who knew them was, too. But, as always, there were a few unrepentant souls who longed for the good old days of torture, poisonings, and assorted mayhem. They were the ones Rollo knew he had to be on the alert for, since they might have aided and abetted the kidnapping. And he knew all of them because he had once been one of them.

But Rollo had changed. He had seen how Chris and Marigold conducted themselves, as monarchs and as people; seen how they got what they wanted by being compassionate, and wise, and funny. And what they wanted were good lives for their subjects. As one of the subjects, he had benefited. Besides, he was about to become a father himself, and he had an idea of how he would feel if anybody stole *his* baby.

At that moment, the baby in question was asleep in the laundry basket inside an old hunter's hut, the kidnappers' rendezvous spot, deep in the forest, not far from the dragon's lair. While the dragon's incinerations could be unpredictable, both Boris and Vlad were too enamored of her to deny themselves the opportunity to be in her vicinity, even though they were on the lam. They figured no one would think they were reckless enough to endanger Poppy, their ace in the hole, by parking her so close to danger. They scoffed at recklessness. Reckless was their middle name. Who but reckless brutes would kidnap a princess? They were *proud* of their recklessness.

The Terrible Twos, Emlyn the laundress, and the two footmen were lounging around, drinking *venti*-size flagons of mead for breakfast, and congratulating themselves on a successful heist.

"No one suspected a single thing about me," Em-

lyn said. "You should have heard me in my job interview with that harridan, Mrs. Clover. She thinks she's
so smart. I fooled her in a second, with all my talk of
lemon juice soaks, and double rinsing, and hot stone
pressing."

"But all that's true," said Bartholomew, the punier
of the two footmen. "You've always worked as a laundress. Your mother and your grandmother were laun-
dresses. You've known all that stuff since you were a
kid. So how is that fooling her?"

"Shut up," Emlyn clarified.

"I'm sure you were brilliant," said Fogarty, the other
footman. "So was I in my interview. I almost matched
the record for running upstairs with a tray of filled wine-
glasses. And I can bow so low, my forehead touches my
knees. I could tell Mrs. Clover was impressed."

Boris and Vlad had had trepidations about leaving
such an important operation in the hands of amateurs,
but being unable to negotiate with any of their old
cohorts due to their own exile, they had had to take
whomever they could find. They gave relieved sighs
that it had gone without a hitch, banged their flagons
together in congratulations, and took big gulps.

"Ah," said Boris, wiping his mouth with his sleeve. "Breakfast of champions."

Vlad winced slightly. Not only was Boris's sleeve wet as well as stained, but his doublet was, too, and he needed a haircut, a bath, and a shave. Vlad knew that being a torturer didn't require as much care and precision as being a poisoner, for whom cleanliness and meticulousness were requirements. One couldn't exactly lick one's fingers after a meal unless one was sure all traces of whatever poison one had been working on were completely washed off, could one? Boris, slovenly Boris, had always gone around with bloodstains on his shirt, his hair a mess, carrying a dirty ax. He said it was important for his image, but Vlad thought he was basically just a slob. Or a showoff.

Vlad, on the other hand, was fastidious about his grooming, with his black hair carefully parted in the center and slicked down with imported hair oil that smelled of licorice. He used it on his mustache, too. He found that it helped obscure the odor of the more disgusting ingredients in several of his poisons.

Though their styles were very different, they had made a good team with ex-queen Olympia. She had been so encouraging of their work and had supplied them with so many victims to experiment on that they still mourned her absence every day. When she was vanquished once and for all, the new king and queen had ascended the thrones and decreed that Olympia's demise meant that Boris and Vlad were to never show their faces in Zandelphia-Beaurivage again. And forget about trying to sneak back in. All the guards would be required to memorize their portraits. King Christian gave the Terrible Twos until sundown that very day to leave for good.

Well! Vlad and Boris could hardly have been more insulted, but they kept their mouths shut while silently vowing revenge. And there was worse to come. Each of their children, who'd always been disappointingly ordinary in spite of the string of brutish and negligent babysitters they'd been tended by, refused to come with them for this permanent exile.

The Terrible Twos had had big plans for Phoebe and Sebastian. They were both meant to be their fathers' successors, to follow in their fetid footsteps. Never mind that Phoebe and Sebastian had always found those footsteps repugnant and hadn't the slightest intention of coming anywhere near them. Boris and Vlad weren't used to hearing the word *no*. And to hear it several times in one day, first from the king and queen and then from their own offspring, was enough to make them wish they had brought some of their most vicious tools of havoc with them to their hearing.

And the reasons Phoebe and Sebastian had given—separately, but so alike—to their fathers! They said *they'd* done nothing wrong, *they* hadn't been ordered into exile, *they* had no interest in torture and poison, and *they* didn't want to have anything more to do with their own fathers, anyway.

What kind of flimsy logic was that?

All this only made the Terrible Twos more determined to get even with the king and queen. And maybe with Sebastian and Phoebe, too.

It had been a long wait, but they had finally done it. And didn't it feel good!

One of the hardest parts of the kidnapping scheme had been deciding what to ask for as ransom. What they really needed was the means to go far away and set themselves up all over again. And finding a new location would not be easy. It was probable they would then need to remove the people filling the positions they would wish to usurp. It could all take time and effort, and be inconvenient. And expensive. So they'd asked for an amount with a lot of zeroes.

It was a great deal more than either of them would have paid in ransom for their own offspring—who were, at that moment, worth exactly nothing to them. But a princess, even a very small one, was certainly worth more than their own ungrateful and defiant progeny, wasn't she?

"So what do we do now?" Emlyn asked. "Just wait?"

Vlad stroked his mustache and sighed. Dealing with flunkeys could be so tedious. How seldom brains and brawn went together.

6

BACK IN THE THRONE room, a sort of hysterical yet
icy calm had descended. Ed, Swithbert, Magnus, and
Wendell were helping Rollo and his men search the
castle while Chris and Marigold tried to think clearly
about what to do next. This was hard to do while they
were suppressing screams.

"Do you know where your fathers went when they
were exiled?" Christian asked Phoebe and Sebastian.

Phoebe shook her head. "Not precisely. But I bet it
wasn't too far away."

"My father always liked the idea of being close to
the dragon," Sebastian said. "They're both pretty big

dragonphiles. And since they weren't ordered specifi-
cally to leave the kingdom—just never to show their
faces here again—I think they stayed deep in the forest, right where they already were. They're lazy. Lots
easier than moving if they didn't have to."

Chris said, "So we should start scouring the forest."

"But carefully," Sebastian said. "We don't want to
push them deeper into hiding."

"Of course. Maybe, instead of stampeding them by
sending Rollo and his guards out, we could go unob-
trusively, just you and me. Who's more motivated than
we are?"

"Me," Marigold said. "You're not going without me."

From the set of her jaw, Chris knew it was useless
to argue, and he'd already made her mad enough. He
nodded and said, "I wouldn't dream of it."

"Or me," Phoebe said. "I'd like nothing better in all
the world than to be there when we catch them. Then
they'll earn a punishment worse than exile, and nobody
would deserve it more."

Sebastian, Chris, and Marigold gaped at Phoebe,
at her furious face and clenched fists. Evidently they

hadn't grasped her full feelings. But now they were way more clear.

"Well," Marigold said. "I guess we *are* the four most motivated people in the kingdom, so we should all be in on it. How soon can we get started?"

"Right away," Christian said. "As soon as we change into some clothing that's warm and dark-colored, and arm ourselves."

Phoebe swallowed hard. She had grown up in a house filled with terrifying instruments—sharp, pointed, and stained with unidentified secretions. She'd vowed never to touch any item designed to do deliberate harm to another person. "No, thank you," she said softly. She knew it wasn't proper etiquette to disagree with the king, but she wasn't going to carry a weapon.

Chris looked into her wide gray eyes so intently that she wondered if he was going to insist. Then he nodded, intuiting her reasons, and said, "All right. Just bring your wits. Sometimes that's the most effective weapon any of us has."

Phoebe blinked away tears. Nobody could have

asked for a wiser, more sensitive monarch than the citizens of Zandelphia-Beaurivage had. With those few words, he had earned her eternal loyalty. She was going to help get baby Poppy back if it killed her.

"We'll meet back here in fifteen minutes, ready to go," the king said, then went off to get ready.

After explaining their reasoning to a disapproving Rollo, who had no choice but to comply, the four of them rode on black horses across the castle's drawbridge into a bleak and chilly landscape. The bulk of the storm had passed on before dawn, but a dreary, unspringlike drizzle still fell, soaking them through. However, they burned with enough outrage and determination that they didn't yet feel the cold.

The horses kicked up great gobs of mud onto their riders as they raced toward the Zandelphia-Beaurivage Bridge, which led to the forests on the Zandelphia side of the river.

Christian knew those forests upside down and backwards. He knew where the dragon's lair was and where the Tooth Fairy's palace was; he knew where the leprechauns minted their gold coins and where the talking trees were. If the Terrible Twos were anywhere near the lair, he would be able to find them, even though the dragon was always an unpredictable obstacle.

After about an hour's worth of riding, Chris halted his horse, and the others stopped beside him. By now they were not only wet, but cold and tired, and some of them (not telling who) were wondering if they were on a wild-goose chase.

"We'll go on foot from here," Chris said. "We're near the dragon, where we suspect the Terrible Twos might be, so we'll have to divide up and quarter the territory. And do it quietly. We don't want them to hear us coming." He gave them their assignments and then said, "We'll meet back here as soon as we've all finished looking around. If you find something, don't try to do anything alone. Come back here and we'll make a plan."

It had all sounded very sensible, even possible, when the king was explaining it. Organized and tidy. But really, when you're slogging around in mud and rain in the gloom of a thick forest, it made no sense at all. It was almost impossible to see anything through the dense trees.

Phoebe floundered and stumbled, not even sure she was still in the section she was supposed to be searching. Her motivation—which had been very high when she was inside a nice warm throne room—was rapidly evaporating. Or maybe freezing was more accurate. Her feet were so cold, she could hardly feel them, and she was soaked through to her underwear.

She blundered ahead a few more muddy feet, tripped over a tree root, and fell against something. At first she thought it was an unusually big tree, but on closer examination, she realized it was a cabin made so cleverly from logs that it appeared to have grown out of the forest floor. Carefully, she felt her way around it, looking for a way to peek inside, stopping from time to time to press her ear against the wall, listening, and hearing nothing. Which could have meant only that whoever was inside was being very careful and very quiet. Every window was completely curtained, which was no help.

But there certainly could be people inside. Phoebe

needed reinforcements. She only hoped she could find her way back to the meeting place, and that there would be somebody there when and if she did.

She did, but there wasn't, not for a long, shivering time. And then everybody came back at once, as bedraggled as she was, and more discouraged.

Through chattering teeth, Phoebe described what she'd found, and hoped that she'd be able to find it again.

"I know exactly what it is," Chris said. "It's that old hunter's cabin that finally got so dilapidated, even hunters wouldn't stay there anymore. I should have thought of it."

"Well, let's go find out. Come on!" Marigold, who had always had a terrible sense of direction, grabbed his hand and began pulling him the wrong way.

"Over here," he said, straightening her out and setting off.

By the time they located the cabin again, the drizzle had stopped, though the trees still dripped so much, it might as well have been raining. Yet there was a little more light to see by.

"We're going to have to open the door, you know,"
Sebastian whispered. "There's no other way to know
what's in there."

Abruptly, Marigold stepped forward and pushed the
door open so hard, it banged against the wall. *At least,*
Phoebe thought, *we know nobody's hiding back there.*
That was small comfort as they all jumped away from
the doorway in case somebody, or something, came
hurtling out.

All was silent.

Marigold peered around the door frame from one
side, and Chris from the other. All was still silent.

Then Marigold took action, marching into the one-
room cabin and yanking the curtain off a window, allowing more light in. "It's empty." Her voice quivered.
"Poppy's not here."

The others entered, looking around at the crude table and chairs, the single rumpled bed, the ashes in the
fireplace.

"But somebody was," Sebastian said. "And not too
long ago, either. There are still a few embers in the
hearth, and there are fresh footprints on the floor."

"And look!" Phoebe bent to retrieve a tiny yellow bootee from under the bed. "Do you recognize this?"

Marigold grabbed it and pressed it to her heart. "It's Poppy's! I knit it for her myself. I recognize all the mistakes I made. I'm not a very good knitter, but I wanted her to have something her own mommy had made. Because I never did."

"Neither did I," Phoebe said quietly.

Chris looked grim and left the cabin. When he came back in, he was shaking his head. "It's too messed up and muddy out there for any good tracks to show. And besides, all of our own footprints have made it even messier."

"We should have brought the dogs!" Marigold exclaimed. "Bub's an excellent tracker. At least he used to be." She felt a wave of remorse at having neglected Bub so badly right up until the moment she needed him. She wouldn't blame him if he didn't even want to help her.

"I'm afraid soft royal living may have blunted his edge," Chris said. "It's been a long time since he's had to track down anything that mattered. And he's older. He may not be as sharp as he once was."

"We have to try!" Marigold exclaimed. "We have to go get him. And the other dogs, too. They're still part of the family, even though I've been so terribly inattentive and neglectful of them." Perhaps it was foolish of Marigold to think that she could make amends to all of the dogs at once. But she also thought, *What could be the harm in trying to kill two birds with one stone?* Or two stones with one bird, as Ed would say.

Lucky for her, the dogs—being more generous and forgiving than people were—would almost certainly take whatever they were offered, be happy with it, and understand the impulse behind it.

They all mounted up and rode back to the castle in a frantic rush. When they got there, they were so covered with splattered mud, the guard at the drawbridge didn't recognize them and almost didn't let them back in. Only after ex-king Swithbert and Rollo had been summoned to identify them were they permitted entry—and the guard spent the rest of that day and the next waiting to be sent to the dungeons for not recognizing his own king and queen. Even though the dungeons were no longer used for their original purpose, those who had lived under the previous regime had not forgotten the punishments that unpredictable monarchs could decree.

Old fears die slowly.

At the same time that Chris, Marigold, Phoebe, and Sebastian were trying to get back into the castle, the Terrible Twos were reminiscing fondly about those good old unpredictable days. If only Olympia were still around, they wouldn't be camping out, crammed together in a leaky tent, with a goat for company. The goat was necessary, to provide milk for the baby, but her hygiene wasn't the finest, making her not the most fragrant tent-mate. Emlyn and Fogarty had tried to convince Boris and Vlad to stay in the hunter's cabin, which, though dilapidated, was at least dry and more spacious than the tent.

But the Terrible Twos had insisted that the cabin was only a temporary measure, a place to assemble and wait out the storm. As soon as the rain let up a little, they needed to get somewhere less obvious, less well-known, and less sneak-up-uponable.

"So now what?" Emlyn asked. "Your ransom note asked for a certain amount—a very *big* amount—but you didn't give any details. How are we supposed to get it?"

"Ah," said Vlad, smoothing his mustache. "That's all part of the plan. The not-knowing builds up anxiety in the distraught parents. We want them ready to agree to any kind of terms, no matter how extravagant or outrageous. We want them in the palms of our hands." As he said that, both he and Boris flexed their hands—his, long and elegant; Boris's square and meaty—as if remembering the good old times when those hands had been busier than they were at the moment.

Poppy lay in the laundry basket, her round brown eyes moving from one face to another.

"Put a blanket over that kid, won't you?" Fogarty said to Emlyn. "I don't like the way she looks at us. Like she's thinking."

Emlyn said, "If she is, she's doing a lot better than you are. But even if she is thinking, what's she going to do about it? She can't walk, or talk, or handle tools. What are you worried about?"

Fogarty draped a blanket over the basket himself. "I just don't like it. It gives me the whim-whams."

As he said that, the goat took a bite out of the back

of his jacket. When he yelped and tore the fabric away, Emlyn laughed, and then said, "Looks like the goat is thinking, too."

Meanwhile, Poppy was wondering why it had suddenly gotten so dark. She'd thought she was figuring out this daytime/nighttime business, but maybe she'd gotten something wrong.

7

Bᴜʙ ᴡᴀs ᴇʟᴀᴛᴇᴅ ᴛᴏ go off to track the Terrible Twos. His feelings had certainly been hurt by the focus on the squalling bundle in the castle, but attention seemed to be on him now, which was good. He didn't want to muff his chance to remind them of what an excellent and irreplaceable dog he had always been. He was a bit put out that Cate, Flopsy, Mopsy, and Topsy would also be coming along in nothing but a decorative capacity; they were all completely useless at tracking and would only be excess baggage. Still, he was used to having them around, so maybe it would work out all right, even if the expedition into the forest was beginning to look like a circus parade.

Bub trotted importantly along beside Chris's horse while Cate rode in the comfort of the king's saddlebag, and Flopsy, Mopsy, and Topsy rode in Marigold's. It was a long trip out to the hunter's cabin; by the time they got there, old Bub was wondering if he would have the stamina to get home again. But he had a job to do and a wish to prove how indispensable he was. Definitely more indispensable than the decorative extra baggage.

He ran around the cabin a few times, his nose a fraction above the mud (most of the time), sniffing like a blacksmith's bellows. Then he sat down and looked up at Chris, his brow furrowed, his ears drooping. Maybe he wasn't so indispensable after all.

"What is it, boy?" Chris asked, as if he expected Bub to answer.

Bub did his best. He shook his head so hard his ears flapped.

"No?" Chris asked. "You're telling me no? No what? No scents? No idea which way they went? No idea what's going on?"

Bub shook his head again and lay down in the mud, looking and feeling mournful. The rain had washed away every scent except that of mud. If it hadn't been so undignified he would have lifted his muzzle and howled in disappointment.

"I think he means he can't do it," Marigold said. "I think this is a dead end."

Suddenly Bub jumped to his feet and began lumbering around in a circle, stiff-legged and moving his head slowly from side to side. Perhaps he could still redeem his reputation and ensure Marigold's affection.

"What's he doing now?" Marigold asked.

"I don't know for sure," Chris said. "You're going to think this is crazy, but it looks to me as if he's imitating Hannibal."

"Hannibal? But why would he want to look like a big white elephant?"

Chris shrugged. "Maybe he thinks Hannibal can help with this somehow."

Marigold just looked at Bub in disbelief, but then decided, *why not?* They were desperate and in a hurry, and why shouldn't Bub know something they didn't about elephants? He spent more time in the stables with Hannibal than she did, that was for sure.

"I wonder if he'll wear dark glasses," Marigold said.

"Who? Hannibal?" Chris asked. "Why would he wear dark glasses?"

"It's an elephant joke," Marigold said. "The answer is, so he won't be recognized." She gave him a weary smile.

"Huh," he said, not appreciating yet another of her jokes. "You don't know how many times I've wished the dogs could talk. I can see how hard he's trying to tell us something, and I can only guess at what it is. What if it's not about Hannibal at all?"

"But I think you're right," Marigold said. "It looks just like him. And even if dogs could talk, most of the time they'd probably just be saying they were hungry."

Chris thought dogs were more complex than that, but he figured this was not a good time to get into that conversation—especially since he thought that whatever dogs had to say, it would be better than an elephant joke.

Bub *woof*ed to get their attention again, then resumed his stiff, swaying walk.

"Yep," Chris said. "That's Hannibal. I guess we have to get him out here with Bub and see what happens."

So once again the group made their way back to the castle through the mud and the oncoming darkness. Halfway there, poor exhausted Bub had to be slung across Chris's saddle and hauled home like a sack of potatoes, while Cate, Flopsy, Mopsy, and Topsy sat perkily in their saddlebags, enjoying the view.

Bub hoped Chris and Marigold had gotten the message that maybe Hannibal, with his huge trunk, would be able to sniff out any lingering, telltale scents that Bub, with only his black, dog-size nose, could not. It was a long shot, he knew, but he was desperate.

Trying to explain to Wendell what they thought Bub wanted wasn't as hard as they thought it would be. Maybe it was because he was a wizard and was used to unusual happenings. Or maybe he knew how eager Hannibal would be to get out of the stables where he had been parked next to the jittery unicorns. Or maybe it was because he was as anxious to find Princess Poppy as anybody was.

"When do you want him?" was all Wendell said.

As much as Christian and Marigold wanted to go back into the forest immediately, they recognized the futility of trying to find anything in the falling darkness, even if they took torches.

"As soon as it's light," Chris said.

And they all went off to spend the night tossing, turning, worrying, and waking suddenly from dreams so awful that they never mentioned them to anyone.

In the morning, they set off again, still without any of the guards but with Hannibal and Wendell. Sebastian was wondering if it was such a hot idea to go out without guards this time, but maybe the king knew best. Maybe all those guards, with their armor and their weapons jangling, would make it too hard to sneak up on the Terrible Twos. Or maybe the king feared the guards would be more interested in attacking than sneaking. Or maybe he feared Poppy could get hurt in a general melee. Still, an expedition that included a great white elephant wasn't the most inconspicuous kind.

"Were you surprised they believed us? When we said we knew it was the Terrible Twos?" Phoebe asked him.

"Sure," Sebastian said. "Weren't you?"

She nodded. "Especially once they knew who we were. But the ransom note confirmed it, so I guess that gave us some credibility. Do you think we'll find the baby?"

"I hope so. Children should be with their mothers."

"Yes," she said wistfully. "What was your mother like?"

"I wish I could remember. One day, when I was three, she went out to gather berries and never returned."

"Really?" Phoebe asked, astonished. "*My* mother disappeared, too. When I was not quite one."

"Maybe it's not so surprising," Sebastian said, "considering who they were married to. Wouldn't *you* want to walk away from them?"

"But our mothers walked away from us, too. Why didn't they take us with them?"

"I've thought about that a lot. And asked my father, too, but he only said he was glad she was gone because she treated me too nicely. So I don't know the answer. There could be lots of reasons. Maybe . . . maybe they didn't go voluntarily. Maybe something befell them. I just don't know."

"What I think about is maybe they didn't want us," Phoebe said in a small voice.

"That could be," Sebastian said. "But I don't want to believe it." For some reason, he felt like comforting her.

"Still. It might be true."

"Here's what I say—when you don't know or can't know the answer to a question, why not believe the answer that you like best? It's as valid as any of the others—and it might be right."

She thought for a moment and then said, "That's brilliant."

"Thank you."

"Did you know that the eye of a duck has three eyelids?"

Every time she told him one of her odd facts, he felt as if she had given him a little present. The only gift he had to give her was his appreciation of the meaning of words. "I did not. You have enlightened me. My interest is always piqued by your pedagogy."

"Really?" she asked, pretty sure she knew what he meant.

"Assuredly."

She flushed with pleasure. "The average cat has twenty-five to thirty whiskers," she murmured.

"That is very good to know," he said.

Wendell joggled along on top of his elephant. He didn't know what Bub thought Hannibal could do, but he didn't question that animals understood each other in ways that people did not, and he trusted Bub's instincts.

He'd been trying to convince Mrs. Clover to take a ride with him on Hannibal, but so far she'd declined the invitation. Come to think of it, he considered, adjusting his awkward seating, it probably wasn't the most comfortable ride in the world. But Hannibal was an advantage he had over Swithbert in the pursuit of Mrs. Clover and he wanted to use all the tricks he had. How else could a washed-up wizard compete with an ex-king?

As they neared the hunter's cabin, Hannibal led them away from it, farther into the forest.

"Isn't this the way to the dragon's lair?" Marigold asked apprehensively. "Why isn't he going to the cabin?"

Here, all the trees had singed leaves and certain sections were beginning to show new growth after being burned to the ground.

"It is indeed," Christian said. A leaden hand seemed to clutch his heart at the idea of his child being anywhere near the dragon. But he knew how the Terrible Twos felt about dragons, so he did what he could to prepare himself for something awful—even though there's actually very little one can do in such a circumstance. There is no such thing as truly being prepared for something awful.

Just then a roar echoed through the forest, followed by a tongue of flame that flickered through the trees ahead of them.

"Uh-oh," Wendell said. He pulled hard on Hannibal's harness, but Hannibal kept going, toward the flames. Wendell pulled harder and yelled, "Stop!" But Hannibal was huge and purposeful, and Wendell had no choice but to go along for the ride.

The rest of the party had halted, and they watched as Hannibal and Wendell headed away. As humorous as the back end of an elephant can be—what with the gigantic rear haunches and the little stringy tail—there was nothing funny about watching their friend being carried helplessly away toward the dragon.

Another spear of flame just missed Hannibal and Wendell, accompanied by another roar. It was becoming increasingly possible that the court crier was going to have some sad and surprising news to report that evening.

8

Up ahead Wendell was beginning to see the scorched earth and charred tree stumps that surrounded the dragon's lair. He smelled charcoal and cooking and was afraid he would soon be part of the aroma. Hannibal kept walking, cinders crunching under his enormous feet, until he was standing on a patch of bare ground. Wendell cringed, his eyes squinched shut, awaiting the flames that would incinerate him. And maybe Hannibal, too, although his skin was thicker and tougher and maybe even fireproof.

It is hard to cringe for very long without getting a kink in one's back and neck, so after a while Wendell had to straighten up and open his eyes. And when he did, he saw that the dragon had come to the mouth of her lair and was looming directly in front of him. It was the first time he had ever been face-to-face with a dragon, and one part of him couldn't help admiring the beautiful iridescence of her scales and the intricate patterns in which they were arranged. The other part of him was afraid his heart had stopped beating for good.

But it started again, and when it did, he noticed that the dragon was paying no attention at all to him.

Her large gold eyes, with surprisingly long and luxurious eyelashes, were fastened on Hannibal, who was just about her size. Her lashes swept down and up again, and a trickle of smoke meandered out of the side of her mouth.

Hannibal raised his trunk and lowered it again, as if in greeting.

Wendell sat, holding his breath, watching his elephant and the dragon watch each other. In the meantime, the rest of the party had edged closer, but not *too* close.

"What do you think is going on?" Marigold asked in a whisper.

"This seems crazy," Chris said. "But it looks to me as if they are—"

"Flirting," Marigold finished for him. "Yes. That's what I thought, too. Can it be? That dragon's probably never seen another creature as big and as—"

"Impressive as she is," Chris cut in. "It's a perfect match."

"What if Hannibal doesn't like her?" Marigold asked. "We don't want him to make her mad."

"Doesn't look to me as if that's happening," Chris said. "He's probably never seen another creature as big and as impressive as he is, either."

"Do you suppose he's lonely?" Marigold asked.

"I never thought about it," Chris said. "But it makes sense. We *should* have thought about it. Poor Hannibal. With only those nervous unicorns for company."

"This could help us," Marigold said.

"Uh, sure," Chris said, not sure at all what she meant.

"If those Terrible Twos are going to try to use the dragon somehow in this, maybe Hannibal can keep that from happening."

"Well, Bub seemed to think we needed Hannibal for something," Chris said. "And he led us straight to the dragon."

"I know I wanted to go back for Bub," Marigold said, lowering her voice. "But he is just a *dog*. I know he's very special to you, but he doesn't really have a record of being brilliant about anything. Except tracking, sometimes."

When Chris sat up straighter, getting defensive about his dog, Marigold remembered about living happily ever after and went on in a more charitable way. "But that doesn't mean he doesn't have some kind of intuition about this situation. He *is* a very sensitive fellow." She hoped she was right about that.

Chris's shoulders relaxed. "I've always believed that animals sense things we can't."

They turned their attention back to the dragon and Hannibal—and poor Wendell, who was both a trapped audience and an innocent bystander to the blossoming romance, if that's what it was.

The dragon had moved a little closer, still trailing a ribbon of smoke from the corner of her mouth. She made a sound, something between a growl and a purr. Hannibal made a low sound in response, but he took one step backward. She frowned and advanced, the smoke increasing in volume and darkening in color.

"Easy, boy," Wendell said to Hannibal. "Don't make her mad. Can't you see she likes you?"

Shafts of angled sunlight struck the scales on the dragon's flanks, causing them to shimmer and glitter with flashes of color. Hannibal raised his great ears in surprise.

"See, Hannibal?" Wendell murmured to him. "Isn't she something? Who else do you know who could do something like that?"

The dragon was all the way out of her lair now, inching across the bare earth toward Hannibal. This time he stood his ground. Her long forked tail rose up over her back and wagged a little, back and forth.

She came right up to Hannibal and bumped his trunk with her nose. He rested the tip of his trunk between her eyes, which she closed. A sigh in the form of a long white plume of smoke issued from her lips.

"This is getting embarrassing," Phoebe said, turning her head. "I feel like we shouldn't be looking. And besides, how is this helping us find Poppy?"

"I think it's sweet," Marigold said dreamily. "Those are two of the rarest and most extraordinary creatures in our world. If they can't help us, I don't know who can. Let's see what else happens."

As they watched, a great tear formed in one of the dragon's eyes and turned to steam as it slid down her face. She lowered her lush lashes and ducked her head as another tear followed, and then a torrent, until her face was almost obscured by a cloud of steam.

Hannibal took a step back and gave her a puzzled look.

"What's happening now?" Chris asked. "Why is she crying? *Is* she crying?"

"I think she's trying to tell him something. And he doesn't know what to do with the news," Marigold replied.

"How in the world do you know that?" Christian asked, astonished.

Marigold shrugged. "Woman's intuition. And remember, I used to be able to read people's thoughts."

"You think she wants him to know something about the Terrible Twos?"

"Possibly. We all know the way they feel about dragons. Maybe they want her to do something she knows is wrong."

"But wait a minute," Sebastian said. "Hasn't she been doing plenty of things wrong? For a long time? Like burning down acres of trees time after time?"

Marigold was quiet for a minute. "You're right," she finally said. "She *has* been doing bad things for a long time. But maybe she had a reason. I can't guess what it would be, but it's possible." Her voice rose. "Do you suppose . . . What if the Terrible Twos hid Poppy in her lair?" Her voice rose higher, became more urgent. "Isn't that the kind of thing Boris and Vlad would do—hide Poppy where nobody would dream of going after her? Could that be why Bub had Hannibal lead us here?" She slid off her horse. "Well, I'm Poppy's mother! I'll go anywhere to get my baby back!" And she picked up her skirts and ran straight toward the dragon's lair.

"Hey!" Chris yelled, jumping off his horse and starting after her.

His shout startled the dragon, who coughed a jet

of flame right at his feet. With the dragon's attention focused on Chris, Marigold ducked under her line of sight and vanished into the lair.

Hannibal raised his trunk and trumpeted with surprise. The dragon looked back at him with the sheepish expression people often have when they are caught doing something they know is wrong, but don't want to admit it. Then she turned her back on Hannibal and Wendell and the rest of them and bustled back into her lair.

"Wait!" Chris yelled as he rushed toward the entrance. "My Marigold is in there!"

Apparently the dragon didn't care. She didn't reappear, and a blast of flames issued from inside.

"Marigold!" Chris cried, dodging the flames. "Marigold! Come out!"

Nothing happened except for more torrents of fire.

Hannibal trumpeted and trumpeted. Finally he faced facts and turned around, lumbering back to where Sebastian and Phoebe waited, their mouths open in astonishment. Not only was Poppy missing, but now Marigold was, too. Instead of making progress, they were going backwards.

Shoulders slumped, Chris led his horse back to them, wisps of smoke rising from his singed doublet. "I can't get in there without getting burned to a crisp. And then who would save Poppy?" He took a deep breath. "I don't know what to do now."

9

"THAT GOAT HAS GOT to go," Emlyn said, holding her nose. "Can't we tie her up outside the tent?"

"You know we tried that," Fogarty said. "Unless she's inside, she bleats so loud she attracts attention we don't want attracted. And she tries to eat the tent."

"Well, then, *I'm* going outside." And Emlyn did just that, saying, "Let me know when you decide anything," as she closed the tent flap. Sitting outside in the mud was better than being in a tent with four men and a goat. She wasn't sure, in fact, which one smelled the worst.

"We need to send that p-mail about the ransom arrangements tonight or first thing in the morning," Vlad said, stroking his mustache in lieu of holding his nose. "I can't take these close living arrangements much longer, either."

"Okay by me," said Boris, who wasn't bothered at all by any number of horrible smells—or unusual body fluids or unearthly shrieks, for that matter. "How shall we do it?"

Vlad said, "I'm formulating a plan. We need to make sure we're in a location where we can't be trapped, and where we can get away easily. That suggests water to me. But we need to make sure we're close enough to the dragon to use her for threat purposes. Even if we can't get her to cooperate. I swear, I never imagined she'd be so stubborn. Wouldn't you think she'd be so flattered at having a poison *and* a torture device named for her that she would be willing to do whatever we asked? But be that as it may, she's still a great *symbol* of a threat. No one has to know she's not cooperating. So . . . let me see . . ." He bent over a strip of paper, scribbling and squinting in the dim light from a candle.

Poppy slept in the laundry basket, her tummy full of goat's milk, dreaming of green meadows populated by large families of happy goats, even though the only goat she had ever seen was one that had been out in the rain and then inside a tent, which hardly ever improves an animal's aroma. Or disposition.

"Is that something you think your fathers might do?" Christian asked Sebastian and Phoebe. "Put a helpless baby in a dragon's lair?" They lingered among the trees within sight of the lair. Chris kept looking over, hoping to see Marigold emerge.

"Well, sure," Sebastian said, wondering why the king was even asking such an obvious question about the inventor of Take Seven Steps and Die. And of Dragon's Sweat, the deadliest poison known to man.

Chris turned to Phoebe, his eyebrows raised in question.

"There's not a doubt in my mind," she said. It seemed unnecessarily cruel, and superfluous besides, to say anything about the glee Boris exhibited when he had a day of torture ahead of him. "But as I think about it more, I don't think he's done that in this case."

After more consideration, Sebastian said, "Neither do I." He and Phoebe looked at each other with a sort of sad acknowledgment. They knew too well how their fathers thought.

"You don't?" Chris asked. "Why not?"

"For one thing, they'd want easy access to the baby for when it's time to exchange her for the ransom," Sebastian said. "And they'd want to be sure they could go in and out of the lair at will, and our dragon seems a bit too unpredictable for that." He wasn't even going to consider the possibility that there would be no baby to exchange for the ransom money, though he knew that the Terrible Twos were more than capable of that sort of thing.

"That makes sense," Chris said. "And you know them. But that means Marigold is stuck in the cave now, in danger, too." He hung his head and rubbed his eyes.

"Yes," Phoebe whispered. "It is a calamitous situation."

Sebastian gave her an admiring look. "Grievous indeed," he whispered back to her.

They watched as Christian stood beside his horse, continuing to rub his eyes, and waited for him to make a kingly decision. It is sometimes easy to forget that a king is still a real person who can make mistakes, and get confused, and become discouraged.

When Chris finally raised his head, he said, "We should go to the hunter's cabin so Hannibal can sniff around. I think that's what Bub wanted him to do. And then we should go back to the castle. I need to send Rollo and his guards out to find and search the forest residences where Vlad and Boris have been living in exile. I should have done that first thing. I thought I was thinking straight, but I was actually panicky. I acted irresponsibly. And on top of everything, I've lost Marigold." He rubbed his eyes again. "I need to sit still for a while and see if I can think straight. And yet I'm afraid of wasting more time."

He shook his head and, without meeting any of their eyes, mounted his horse and rode off the way they had come, back to the hunter's cabin—where Hannibal sniffed and sniffed with his great big sniffer but could find nothing that Bub hadn't.

It was a silent and dejected group that arrived back at the castle. Christian left his horse at the stables, gave Rollo his orders, and went off alone, to close himself up in his private chambers. Wendell, in need of cheer, passed through the castle corridors, looking for Mrs. Clover. To his dismay, she was busy having a cup of tea and a lovely long conversation in the kitchen with Denby, Swithbert's valet. And Phoebe and Sebastian went their separate ways, to the blacksmith shop and the library, after several backward glances that weren't coordinated enough to allow either to know that the other one was looking.

They were all back in the throne room early the next morning (along with Ed, Swithbert, and Magnus, who were anxious to know how things were progressing), just as a little light from the false dawn was beginning to seep through the high stained-glass windows.

Chris brought them up to date. "Rollo and the guards were heroic. They searched most of the night until they finally found Vlad's and Boris's places, way out in the forest, past the dragon. But they were deserted. They searched them top to bottom but found nothing to indicate where the Terrible Twos might be now."

Before he could go on, a page came running in, a

pigeon in his hands. "Sire, this p-mail just arrived." He thrust the pigeon at Chris.

With trembling fingers, Chris opened the container on the pigeon's leg and shook out the strip of paper inside. "'Do you want your daughter back?'" he read aloud, then murmured, "What a stupid question."

"Sounds more like Boris than Vlad," Phoebe said.

Chris read on. "'Bring the two million ducats to the dragon's lair. Tomorrow at sunset.'"

"Those snakes in the grass are barking up the wrong tree, if they think they can get away with this," Ed said, his fists clenched in anger.

Chris raised his head. "Two million ducats is almost everything Marigold and I have earned from my inventions and her perfume business. But we'd spend it all, and more, to get Poppy back. How fast can we bag it up?"

"I think we can just about make it," Swithbert said, "if we start right now." He jumped up as fast as his crotchety knees would allow. "Magnus, you come with me. We'll get Mrs. Clover and Denby to supervise the servants who'll be doing the bagging. They're the most reliable staff members we have. We don't want to take any chances on anybody putting a few ducats in their pockets. We're going to need every one for the ransom." He and Magnus hurried out.

"Your Highness," Sebastian said. "I know you're more than willing to hand over the money. But that deadline gives us two days to keep looking. We don't have to give up yet."

"I agree," Ed said. "I'm throwing a cold blanket on giving up right now."

Chris put one hand on Sebastian's shoulder and one on Ed's. "You two don't quit, do you? I'm out of ideas. Do either of you have any?"

Ed shook his head. "I wish I did, but I'm afraid you have to include me out."

"I've been thinking about it," Sebastian said. "What I've come up with may not be as true for Boris as it is for my father, but Vlad likes his comforts. He can rough it for a couple of days, and then he's sick of it. He wants a good bed and some privacy and something decent to eat. I believe he would have hidden out with little Princess Poppy right at first, when it would have been logical for you to search for his house, but once he thought you'd moved on, he'd be wanting to get back home."

Chris sighed. "It *would* have been logical to search there first, wouldn't it? But I didn't do that. However, as of last night, he still wasn't there. Do you think he's there now? With Poppy?"

"What can it hurt to look again? We don't want to miss them."

"Excuse me, Your Highness," Phoebe said. "We should probably look in Boris's house, too. They could be there. They *have* spent a lifetime working together. Though I'd put money on a bet that it's nowhere as nice as Vlad's place."

"That would be my guess, too," Chris said. He had gained a sense of Phoebe's childhood, living with a feared and reviled parent with a reputation of being a slob, in an unkempt, motherless home. "Well, let's not waste any more time."

"Right," Ed said. "Go get them! You've taken a big headache off my shoulders."

10

"AAAH," VLAD SAID, STRETCHING out in his favorite chair, his feet up on his favorite footstool (a stuffed snapping turtle), a glass of thistle juice spiked with fermented frizzer (a pretty potent combo) in his hand. "Don't I deserve this! After sleeping in a tent! With a goat! Waiting for Rollo and his troop of oafs to finally do what I'd expected them to do a lot sooner—quit pawing through my things and ride back to Beaurivage Castle. The things I put up with for a fortune!"

Boris sprawled on the weasel-fur rug in front of the fire, trying to get his mouth around a gigantic anaconda-sausage sandwich. "I wish I could unhinge my jaw, the way this snake could have done," he said.

"Then I wouldn't have any trouble at all." Finally, he just stuffed the sandwich in, causing chunks to tumble down his shirt and onto the floor.

"It won't be long before I can upgrade," Vlad mused, giving Boris a look of disgust. "After this caper is over, I'm on my way to greener pastures. Once word gets out about this heist, I'll be in demand in any number of places. When that money's in my hands, I'm history."

"Me, too," Boris mumbled around his sandwich.

"Old boy," Vlad said. "Let me suggest something. For your future. I believe you should begin planning on one without me."

"One what?" Boris mumbled.

"Future. It's been a long and fruitful partnership but I rather think it's time for us to be going our separate ways now."

"What!" Boris exclaimed, then coughed, a piece of anaconda-sausage stuck in his throat.

"Yes," Vlad went on calmly, watching Boris's face get redder and redder. "I need to move on unhindered by any baggage."

Boris gasped and gargled, his eyes bugging out, his

lips forming what might have been the words, "Help! I'm choking!"

Vlad regarded him placidly.

Boris had rolled onto his back and was writhing desperately when Emlyn entered the room. "Lucifer's lunchbox!" she exclaimed. "Look at Boris!" She ran to him, pulled him into a sitting position, and hugged him hard from behind. The thrust of her hug caused a hunk of sausage to shoot from Boris's mouth and smack into the wall, missing Vlad by inches. Vlad raised the corner of his lip in repugnance.

Boris scrambled to his feet and charged, yelling, "Were you just going to watch me choke to death?" He closed his hands around Vlad's throat. Now it was Vlad's turn to turn several shades of red.

"Hey!" Emlyn shouted, grabbing Boris's hands. "I don't care what you two do to each other once we've got the ransom money. But let's keep it together until then, okay? We're going to have enough trouble with other people trying to hurt us without doing it to each other." She yanked hard at Boris and managed to pull him off Vlad.

Boris lay on the floor at Emlyn's feet, gasping, while

Vlad, his hands protectively around his throat, gasped, too.

"You were going to watch me expire," Boris wheezed.

"Of course not," Vlad said, then coughed. "I would have gotten to you in time to save you."

"Hah!" Boris said bitterly.

"Well, thanks to Emlyn"—and Vlad gave her a dark look—"now you'll never know for sure."

"Me?" Emlyn squealed, getting the idea that she had interrupted something more malign than an accidental choking. "I was just responding to an emergency, the way any sensible person would do." No one seemed to find any irony in an accomplice to a felony regarding herself as a sensible, compassionate person.

"And what did you mean about going our separate ways?" Boris went on. "What am I supposed to do on my own?"

"I believe you have certain marketable skills," Vlad said, adjusting his collar. "Rather crude ones, I would admit, but ones that have stood you in good stead. All you have to do now is to find another monarch who values the art of torture as much as Queen Olympia did."

"And where am I supposed to find that?" Boris blustered. "You think I can just walk into any random kingdom and ask if anyone needs to have their fingers broken by the Digit Snapper? Or the flesh of their faces flayed by the Dragon's Teeth?"

"I would suggest more subtlety than that," Vlad said.

"Hey, wait a minute," Boris said, his eyes narrowing. "You've been thinking about this for a long time already, haven't you? You've made your plans without consulting me, or even telling me. You don't want me with you, do you?"

Vlad rolled his eyes, as if to say, *The poor numbskull is finally getting the picture.* "I believe it would be best for our individual careers and reputations if we forged separate identities. You'd want that, wouldn't you? Why would you want your name attached to mine, in case I were to do something stupid?"

"I think you just have," Boris said, baring his teeth.

"Now, now," Vlad said soothingly. "Let's be sensible. By tomorrow we'll be wealthy men again, ready to begin anew after years of humiliation and disgrace. You have to admit that our prospects in this kingdom are finished. We have to move on. And our possibilities are greater as individuals than as a team."

"I don't know what makes you say that. We have a reputation as a team."

"And what makes you think that? Isn't it just as logical that we have two different reputations?"

"Hey!" Emlyn interrupted. "Boris! Can't you get that he doesn't want to work with you anymore? When somebody doesn't want you, arguing with him is not going to change his mind. Believe me, I know. It's the same with boyfriends."

Boris looked at the floor, his brow furrowed. "I've never had to look for a job before. I just followed in my father's torturing footsteps. I don't know how to do it."

"Think of it as a learning opportunity, then." Vlad sprang from his chair and paced briskly. "It's important, I believe, to keep our minds agile and flexible by providing them with new experiences. Approach this occasion with optimism. With enthusiasm. With zest!"

Boris's head lowered further between his hunched shoulders. "Right. Zest."

"Oh, for the love of—" Emlyn began. "What kind of a pantywaist have I gotten mixed up with? I thought you guys were pros."

"We are, we are," Vlad insisted. "By tomorrow, when we collect those two million ducats, you'll know that for sure. And we'll all feel better about moving on with our lives. You'll see. And you, Emlyn—what are your future plans?"

"How many families do you think would want to hire me after it's apparent that I can't get a reference from my previous employer?"

"Have you never heard of forged references?" Vlad asked silkily.

"What a great idea!" Emlyn exclaimed. "Why, that way I can be the best employee they ever heard of. I'll be in demand!"

"Now you're talking," Vlad said, pleased. "That's the kind of initiative I like to see. Boris? Are you paying attention? You could take a lesson from this girl. Nobody's as interested in your future potential as you are. Nobody else will work as hard to see that you get ahead. Are you getting the picture?"

Miserably, Boris nodded.

"Sheesh!" Emlyn exclaimed, and left the room.

Christian set off with Sebastian, Phoebe, Wendell (you never knew when you might need a wizard), Hannibal (where Wendell went, Hannibal went, too), Rollo, and three of the guards who had been with Rollo when they found Vlad's residence. They rode through the forest, the only sound that of their mounts' hooves crushing the leaves and twigs on the ground. Hannibal's big feet just made bigger crushing sounds.

As they approached the vicinity of the dragon's lair, the elephant slowed down and turned his head, his huge ears stretched out like sails, as if trying to catch the slightest sound coming from the lair. Perhaps he did, because he came to a complete stop and lifted his trunk, sniffing.

Christian felt as if his own ears, too, were stretched, listening for some sound indicating Marigold's presence. He halted the procession and waited. He had come to believe that Hannibal sensed things that humans did not, and he didn't want to interfere. He also didn't want to interfere with any possibility that Hannibal could be instrumental in rescuing Marigold, as well as finding Poppy. He still hoped that Bub might have been on to something by wanting Hannibal in on the search. Besides, he remembered what the early stages of falling in love had felt like, and he recognized them in Hannibal—especially that desperate desire to be near the one you love.

Hannibal trumpeted once and then waited, his ears cocked. Chris wanted to believe that Hannibal understood the importance of a silent surprise approach to Vlad's abode, but Chris himself also understood the need to communicate with a distant beloved. His own beloved was somewhere over there, he hoped, and he would have trumpeted, too, if he could.

Above the trees, a plume of white smoke coalesced into the shape of a perfect heart before it dissipated into wisps and trails. Surely that had not been an accident. Apparently Hannibal didn't think so, either. He gave a satisfied little *toot* and then seemed willing to proceed.

Chris was reluctant to go on without mounting a vigorous search for Marigold, but risking combustion by the dragon would help no one. He knew the queen well enough to be certain that she would be with him if she could be. And he knew she would say that his first duty was to find their little Poppy. Once that was done, he could come back for her, and together they would figure out a way to get them all safely home.

What he could do right now was to leave two of Rollo's troops near the lair, ready to assist Marigold if it became necessary.

Christian sighed, sent some warm and encouraging thoughts in Marigold's direction, and urged the search party onward. He nurtured a hope that the dragon's heart-shaped feelings for Hannibal would translate into kinder treatment for Marigold and any other captives she might be harboring, despite the dragon's well-earned reputation for pyromania.

They rode for a long time, deeper and deeper into the forest.

Closer to Vlad's abode, they dismounted and tied up their horses and Hannibal. Clutching their weapons, they began to creep through the trees. Wendell was glad Christian hadn't decided they should run. If any wizardry was necessary, he needed to have all his strength.

"What kind of weapon is that?" Chris whispered to Sebastian.

"I call it an Arthurian mace. I made it up from scraps in the blacksmith's shop."

"I made a flying machine once from scraps," Chris said. "It's fun, isn't it, inventing things?"

"Indeed it is, Your Majesty. I'd say it's my hobby as well as my employment. I must admit, I feel rather guilty inventing a weapon. My father used poison as a terrible weapon, and I never want to be like him in any way."

"Weapons can be necessary for self-defense," Chris assured him. "It's all in how we use what's given to us. Would you mind if I had a look at your mace?"

Of course one never says *no* to one's monarch, so Sebastian handed the mace right over and took the king's halberd in return. Christian hefted the mace. "It's beautifully balanced," he said. "And very heavy." He ran his hand over the head of it. "And this design along the shaft—it's almost too beautiful for a weapon." He handed it to Rollo, who silently admired it and wondered if he could get Sebastian to make one for him.

"I tried to imagine the kind of design King Arthur would have," Sebastian said modestly.

"Big admirer of his, are you?" Chris held up his hand, bringing the party to a halt behind a screen of bushes not far from the lodge.

"Yes, I am, Your Highness. He was a wise and strong leader, and one who suffered a great heartache with dignity." Sebastian shut up then, afraid the king might think he was being compared unfavorably to the great mythic Arthur. How he wished he'd had a father like Arthur, who was wise and strong and possessed of a heart that could be touched. Many times Sebastian had been unsure that Vlad even *had* a heart.

"I agree," Chris whispered. "I aspire to be the kind of king he was. I even have a wonderful model of King Arthur and his knights seated at the Round Table. I bought it at a Market Day stall to inspire me. I must show it to you sometime."

"Thank you, sire," Sebastian replied faintly. "Would you like your halberd back before we go in? Or would you prefer to try my mace?"

Christian took the mace from Rollo and handed it back to Sebastian. "I'd never make a raid with an unfamiliar weapon. But I'd like you to instruct me in how to use it someday soon. Would you?"

"It would be my pleasure," Sebastian said.

"Now let's go get Poppy." Chris rose from the crouch he was in and, brandishing his halberd, began running toward Vlad's lodge. The others followed.

Wendell struggled to keep up, glad he probably wouldn't have to run very far.

11

At THAT VERY MOMENT, Bartholomew, the younger footman, was looking out the window of the lodge, wondering how in the world he had ever let Emlyn talk him into helping her kidnap the baby princess. It was true that Emlyn was his cousin and had always pushed him around, and also that he was afraid to say no to her because she gave painful wrist-burns and lip-twists, especially since she'd started hanging out with Fogarty, who was even meaner than she was.

He'd thought he was safe when he'd left his home village and gotten a job at the castle. He loved his work on the household staff, fetching things for the royal family, keeping Swithbert's cup filled while he played endless games of Snipsnapsnorum, running errands. It was easy and satisfying work with nice people, and he had been happy. He couldn't believe his eyes when Emlyn and Fogarty showed up at the castle as employees! And Emlyn was to work as the nursery laundress! She was the last person who should be allowed around a baby.

And then kidnapping! With Vlad and Boris, the Terrible Twos! What had possessed him? What could Emlyn have done to him that would be worse than what would happen to him if he got caught?

Miserably, Bartholomew looked out the window, wondering how hard it would be to sneak away from this disaster. And what he saw made him change his thought from *if* he got caught to *when* he got caught! Here came the king! Running! Armed with a very pointy six-foot-long halberd and with some followers, including a guy carrying a weapon he'd never seen before, the captain of the guards, that wizard who had the big elephant, and the librarian.

Bartholomew didn't know what to make of this assortment, but he was sure it wasn't good news for him.

No way was he sticking around to see how this turned out. He was *going!*

As he dashed out into the hallway, he bumped into Fogarty, holding a rope attached to the goat. Behind Fogarty ran Emlyn, with the baby in the laundry basket, Vlad, and Boris.

"Where are you going?" Bartholomew cried.

"Out of here!" Emlyn yelled as they all disappeared around a corner. "There's trouble on the way!"

I know! Bartholomew thought, but he yelled after Emlyn, "When were you going to tell me?"

There was no answer, and he found himself standing alone in the hall. Only when he heard the front door blast open did he leap into action, running through the back exit just in time to see Fogarty, Emlyn, Vlad, and Boris vanish into the trees. The goat stood alone, munching contentedly on a patch of creeping quack grass.

"Hey!" he hollered. "You forgot the goat! The baby needs the goat!"

The last flashes of running felons were swallowed up by the forest. And as that happened, Bartholomew realized that they had abandoned the goat because they no longer intended to feed the baby. They were going to collect the ransom and scatter. They might be, at this very instant, abandoning the little princess somewhere in the thick darkness of the tangled underbrush.

He was still standing there, the goat's rope in his hand, when the king and the others came piling out the back door of the lodge, bristling with shiny, sharp weapons.

"Hey, you!" Christian yelled. "Did you see some people come out this way?"

Dumbly, Bartholomew nodded and pointed into the trees.

"Come on!" The king waved his little posse onward. "They can't be very far ahead!" And he ran off into the forest, followed by the others, while Bartholomew stood watching them, still holding the goat's rope.

Is it going to be that easy? he thought. Had no one recognized him? Was he going to be able to go back to the castle with some elaborate excuse for why he'd been missing for three days, bringing a goat along for amends, while Vlad and Boris, Emlyn and Fogarty, got whacked, and the baby rescued? But what if they only got captured and taken to the dungeon? They'd blab about him, for sure. Maybe his best option was just to run. But where would he go? And how fast could he move towing a goat? Wait—did he need to take the goat?

Bartholomew stood, immobilized by indecision, while the goat went back to enjoying the creeping quack grass. When he felt a tap on his shoulder, he jumped so hard that he yanked the rope, sending a wad of partly chewed quack grass shooting out of the goat's mouth. When he whipped around, there was the librarian, with her hands on her hips, glaring at him

"Don't give me that stupid, innocent look," she said. "I know you're in on this."

"In? In on w-what?" he stammered, feeling completely stupid if not all that innocent.

"I know who you are. Do you think that because I work in the library and hardly anybody ever talks to me that I don't know what goes on in the castle? The library window is right above one of the most popular stalls on Market Day—the one that sells all the clever gadgets and the Camelot miniatures. People stand there forever looking at things and gossiping. I hear it all. I know your cousin was the laundress for the baby princess. I know you're not the sharpest dagger in the arms chest. Well, I *am*. That's why I stayed behind the others, to see if the Terrible Twos had left behind any tricks or clues. I guess you're it. So where's the baby?"

"Baby?" he babbled. "What baby?"

She removed the sash from around her waist and snapped it between her hands. "I'm not in the mood for this. And in case you think I don't know how many ways to use this sash to inflict damage"—she gave the sash another snap—"please remember that I grew up in a house full of instruments of torture that only a twisted mind could ever think up. And I know how every one of them works." She didn't add, of course, that the very idea of using instruments of torture made her want to weep, and that all she knew about her sash was how to tie it around her waist. One needs to keep one's advantage, after all.

Bartholomew fell to his knees and hugged Phoebe around the ankles. Because he was still holding on to the goat's rope, she found herself not only immobilized by his grip, but in much closer proximity to a goat than she cared to be. The goat took a mouthful of sash as Bartholomew wailed, "I didn't want to! But I've always been afraid of Emlyn. And she was mixed up with Boris and Vlad, and she threatened me with what they'd do to me if I didn't help. I was afraid of them all! I'm a dope, and a coward, and a weakling. I admit it. But I never wanted to harm the baby! They said they'd bring her back once they had the ransom money. But now I know they're not going to! Because of the goat." He put his head down on her shoes and sobbed.

"The goat?" Phoebe asked. Maybe she wasn't so smart, she thought, or maybe he was even duller than she'd thought he was. She wasn't following this. What did the goat have to do with anything?

"For milk for the baby. They didn't take the goat."

Then she got it, and her heart felt chilled. "Get up!" she ordered. "We've got to find them now! Where were they going?"

Painfully, Bartholomew got to his feet. "I don't know.

They were just running. And they left me behind." He hiccupped.

"Do they have a backup hiding place? They're still planning to collect the ransom money at the dragon's lair tomorrow, right? So they can't go far."

"I don't know. They never told me anything. I was just supposed to make sure doors that should have been locked were left open, and that the coast was clear, and that I tied up Mrs. Sunday while they got the baby. They *used* me!" And more tears oozed from his eyes.

"Oh, stop that," Phoebe said impatiently. Did he really think she would feel sorry for a bonehead like him who had abetted such an awful outrage? "Get moving. We have to find the others and tell them what's going on."

"But *why* can't we go hide out at my place?" Boris implored, panting as they hustled through the trees. "It's not far. And we got to hide out at *your* place." He sounded quite petulant about that.

"And you think your place won't be the first place

they'll look after my lodge? They weren't supposed to double-check mine, but they did. So why wouldn't they go back to yours?" Vlad asked scornfully. "Besides, yours is a pigsty."

"Hey!" Boris responded, stung.

"So where are we going to hide?" Emlyn asked. "We left the tent behind."

"This wasn't part of the plan," Vlad said. He'd been running as fast as the rest of them, but he didn't sweat or even seem to be out of breath. "And we're going to have to make sure there's no crying to give us away."

"I'm not going to be crying," Emlyn said, insulted. "I never cry."

"Me neither," Boris said, gasping for breath.

"You mean me?" Fogarty asked. "I won't cry."

"Must you all demonstrate your deficiencies?" Vlad asked. "Who else do we have with us?"

"Oh!" Boris said. "The baby. But she never cries."

"That doesn't mean she won't. She's a *baby,* or have you forgotten what we're doing here?"

Fogarty looked behind him as they ran. "Where's Bartholomew? I left the goat for him to bring. *I* didn't want to be dragging that thing along. She keeps eating my pants."

"Don't worry about it. We're not going to need the goat. We're only going to have this kid with us for another day, until the ransom is paid. I have ways to keep her quiet until then."

"But Bartholomew," Fogarty continued. "What happened to him? They could catch him."

"Even if they do, he can't tell them anything. He doesn't *know* anything—in more ways than one. And he'll keep them busy, slow them down, while we get away. How fast do you think we could have gone with a goat, anyway?"

"What do you mean you have ways to keep her quiet?" Emlyn asked. Hardhearted as she was, she hadn't been immune to Poppy's good nature or the charm of the adorable little royal baby garments that she'd spent so much time laundering.

"Have you forgotten I'm a scientist?" Vlad asked. "I can whip up a sleeping potion with one arm tied behind my back."

The only sleeping potions Emlyn had known to come out of Vlad's laboratory were ones that made someone sleep permanently. "Do you mean actual *sleep?*" she asked. "Or . . ." She trailed off.

Vlad ignored her and kept going, weaving sinuously between the trees. They plunged on, following him until he came to a halt at a jumble of rocks that looked as if they'd been tossed around by a giant's hand. Maybe they had been.

"Ah," he said. "This will do."

"What?" Fogarty asked. "What will do?"

"You know this whole area is riddled with caves, don't you?" Vlad said. "The dragon lives in one. That great big, crystal-studded one is now the Zandelphia castle. They're all over the place. And I'm betting there's one in here. One that will be hard to find—though not for me, of course—because of the disorder of these rocks." He climbed up into the rock pile and began poking around while the rest of them sank onto the ground, panting.

"If he's so smart, why are we in this mess?" Fogarty said. "I thought this was supposed to be a straight, uncomplicated job. Take the kid, get the money, give the kid back."

"So did I," Emlyn said. "Maybe this is just a little

hitch. After tomorrow we'll have our money and it'll be over." But her voice didn't sound as confident as she wished it had.

"What about it, Boris?" Fogarty asked. "What do you think?"

Thinking wasn't something Boris was all that familiar with, but he wrinkled his brow and gave it a try. He had spent his life building instruments of torture and using them. That was easy, unlike thinking. Since the exile, he'd been rootless and restless, desperate for something to do, but he hadn't been able to figure out what. And he was running out of money, besides.

This kidnapping idea of Vlad's had seemed like the answer to a prayer. Some excitement, some vengeance on the people who had ruined his life, a lot of money at the end of it, and the opportunity to relocate, to find a place where he and Vlad could use their skills again. But somehow it all seemed to be going horribly wrong. No one had ever mentioned anything about a tent, or a goat, or running for one's life. Or about being abandoned by Vlad, his lifetime accomplice. Boris's home in exile might be a pigsty—really, he didn't think it was *that* bad—but it was familiar, and he wished he was in it right now.

"Well, I . . ." he began, not sure what he was going to say. But before he could go any farther, Vlad exclaimed, "I've found it! Come here!"

They all began scrambling over the rocks, passing the laundry basket containing Princess Poppy from hand to hand as they hustled to where Vlad waited. But they couldn't see any opening to a cave.

"You found what?" Boris asked, wiping sweat from his eyes with the tail of his shirt.

"Look." Vlad pointed. "Down there."

They looked. At their feet was a small hole, barely visible under an overhanging rock.

"Oh, no," Fogarty said. "I'm not going down there. It looks like there's only one way in or out. That's never smart. Didn't you say we should hide somewhere we couldn't be trapped, and where we could get away easily? And didn't you say we should be near water? This has none of that."

"And it's *dark*," Emlyn said. "How can you make a sleeping potion in the dark?"

"I'm not sure I'll fit in there," Boris added. "It's a pretty small hole, and I've put on a bit since I haven't been working." He patted his round stomach. "And we don't know how big the space is. Will we all fit?"

"One must be adaptable," Vlad said. "Those are all reasons that it's the perfect hiding place. There's only one way in, so no one can sneak up on us. And if they try to get in, they're perfect targets. Yes, it's dark, but that makes it safe. And I already have the sleeping potion. I brought it here with me from my lodge. As for you, Boris, I'm sure we can get you in if we push hard enough. And we'll all fit inside, even if I have to have Boris lop off a few parts."

These arguments were met with silence. Especially the last one. Finally Emlyn said, "What if they find us and don't even try to get us out? What if they just cover the hole with rocks and go away?"

Fogarty gulped loudly.

"Don't forget," Vlad said smoothly. "We have the baby. They'd never do that as long as we have her."

Again they were silent. And Emlyn was again the one to speak. "What if it *is* too small for all of us?"

Just then, behind them and above the treetops, a flock of widgeons suddenly took flight, as if startled by something. Like maybe a king and his followers on the chase.

"Anybody have a better idea?" Vlad asked.

Another flock of widgeons, a little closer, erupted over the treetops.

"Well?" he prodded.

Fogarty sighed heavily, then said, "Oh, all right," and lowered himself into the hole.

"You next, Emlyn," Vlad said. "Chop-chop. They're getting closer."

Reluctantly, Emlyn followed Fogarty down into the hole. Once she landed, she called up, "It's deeper than I thought down here. And darker."

"You next, Boris," Vlad said, holding the laundry basket containing the princess under his arm.

Boris, whose brain cells had been piqued by some of Fogarty's and Emlyn's comments, felt a crowd of question marks arriving in his mind. Could Vlad be trusted? Come to think of it, he'd never known him to be especially trustworthy.

"That's okay," Boris said. "You go ahead. I'll hand the basket down to you."

"I insist," Vlad insisted.

"How come you're so insistent?" Boris asked. "Why don't you want to go first?"

"What's going on up there?" Emlyn called.

Vlad said, "I can't go first because someone will need to give you a push to get you through. Now move it! Time's wasting!"

"You can pull on my legs from down there to get me in," Boris said. "Now I'm insisting." He flexed his thick biceps and scowled.

Vlad took a long look at Boris, his brows drawn together in contemplation, then turned on his heels and sprinted off, clambering over the rock pile and vanishing down the other side.

"Huh?" Boris said, before realizing that Vlad had never had any intention of going down into the hole. He was escaping! With the object of the ransom! That baby was worth two million ducats and Vlad was getting away with her!

With a spurt of adrenaline, Boris took off after him.

"Hey!" Emlyn yelled from the bottom of the hole. "Where is everybody else?"

The only sound she heard was the rattle of stones under Boris's boots as he hustled up over the rock pile, hot on Vlad's trail.

12

I KNOW THEY CAME THIS way!" Chris called back as he ran. "I didn't spend my childhood in these woods without knowing how to track."

They had had to stop while Wendell caught his breath. Chris wished he could have kept the group running off without Wendell, but it had been his idea to bring the wizard on this expedition, so he was forced to have them all accommodate. If they'd only reached Vlad's lodge a few minutes sooner, he'd have Poppy now, safe and sound (he hoped), and Boris and Vlad and their cohorts would be in custody. Why hadn't they started earlier, ridden faster, dawdled less? But now he was so close behind, he could almost smell them. Or maybe he actually *was* smelling Boris, who had always left quite an aroma in his wake.

Sebastian, Rollo, and the other guard stayed alert to make sure they weren't set upon—either by the kidnappers or any other random rogues who frequented the forest. And as Sebastian looked around, he noticed something.

"Where's Phoebe?" he asked. "When did we lose her?"

"She was behind me when I ran out the back door," Wendell said, proud that he had been going fast enough to be ahead of *someone*. "But I don't recall seeing her since then."

"Neither do I," Chris said, rising from where he'd been examining the trail. He knew now which way the culprits had gone and he was eager to keep going.

Sebastian wondered how he could have taken this long to notice she was missing, when he was usually conscious of her every move. "I'll go back," he said, alarm in his voice. "Something must have happened to her."

Just then they heard a call through the dense forest.

"It's Phoebe!" Sebastian said, running back the way they had come. "It's Phoebe!"

It took longer than Christian had hoped it would, but soon Sebastian returned to the clearing, holding Phoebe by the hand. She was followed by a goat on a rope, and in her other hand she held her sash, the opposite end of which was bound around the wrists of Bartholomew.

"What's this?" Christian asked.

Phoebe gave him a quick explanation. The presence of the goat, once the king understood it, caused his heart to grow cold.

"We've got to find them," Chris said. "We've *got* to. Wendell, I want you and the guardsman and Hannibal to head back to the castle with the goat and Bartholomew. I'll deal with him later. Right now, we've got to move faster."

Wendell grumbled about being left behind, but truthfully, he was glad. His legs were old and short and he'd run about as far as he could. "All right. As long as you know I wish I was coming with you. But I'll do my duty. Come on, you." He pulled the goat behind him while the guard took hold of Bartholomew.

Chris turned to the young footman. "And in case you're getting any ideas, Wendell is an accomplished wizard and he can turn you into a toad in an eye blink if there's any funny business."

Wendell wasn't entirely sure he *could* do that, but the king's stern voice was apparently convincing, because Bartholomew muttered glumly, "It might be better if he did. I'm pretty much a toad already."

"Come on, then," Wendell said, and he and the guard dragged their captives off through the trees.

When Wendell, Bartholomew, and the goat were out of sight, Sebastian said, "Pardon me, Your Majesty. I don't mean to be insubordinate, but do you think it's wise to send Wendell off, even if he is a wizard? Bartholomew is twice as big as he is, and younger and stronger. He'd have no trouble overpowering Wendell if he took it into his mind to do so."

"I don't mind your questioning me at all, Sebastian," Christian said. "It's the duty of a conscientious citizenry. But don't worry about Wendell. Even if his powers are diminished—and I think I convinced Bartholomew they aren't—he's as tough as ten ice bears and has a heart of iron. Bartholomew wouldn't have a chance. Besides, there's a very well-armed guard with them."

Phoebe was thinking, *Insubordinate. What a lovely word.* And when was the last time she'd heard a nice-looking young man use it? Why—never, that's when. What a treat. And to have a ruler who could say *conscientious* and *citizenry* in the same sentence. Lovely.

With that, Christian turned back into the forest and once again picked up the trail of the kidnappers.

Emlyn and Fogarty each reacted differently to being left deep in the hole. Fogarty, to his own surprise, burst into furious tears. And Emlyn scooped up all the rocks she could find and hurled them out of the hole, even though she knew the Terrible Twos were long gone and couldn't be touched by them. She also yelled every bad word she had ever heard, taking some satisfaction in hearing them echo in the dimness. She hated to admit it, but she was as worried about the fate of Poppy as she was outraged at being so easily hornswoggled. She should have known better than to trust Vlad when it came to dividing up a lot of money. Of course he would try to get rid of his cohorts.

"How long do you think we'll be in here?" Fogarty whined.

"How should I know?" Emlyn said crossly. "Maybe forever."

Forgarty burst into fresh torrents of weeping.

"Oh, shut up," Emlyn comforted. "We need to figure a way to get out of here."

"There is no way without someone to help us," he sobbed. "We have no tools, no equipment. Nothing."

"You make a very good point," Emlyn said. "Thanks for the helpful information. I think maybe I could get out if you would let me stand on your shoulders."

"Then how will *I* get out?"

"I'll go get a rope," she said brightly.

"Nothing doing. I know you well enough to know you'd never come back. So why should I help you escape?"

He was smarter than she'd hoped. Folding her arms across her chest, Emlyn plopped down on the damp ground. "Since you're so smart, *you* come up with a plan."

They sat in grim silence, stewing and fuming and weeping helplessly.

There are only a few things worse than having to face up to the fact that the predicaments one finds oneself in are usually the results of one's own foolish actions.

Chris powered on through the trees, his mind on Poppy, and also on Marigold, trapped in the dragon's lair with no way out. He'd have to worry about that later, though. Right now, he had to get Poppy back before those Terrible Twos starved her, or abandoned her someplace where he'd never find her.

Abruptly he came to a halt against a great tumbled pile of rocks.

"Looks like a giant's been playing here," Chris said. "But here's something I know about giants' playgrounds. Giants leave deep footprints. Big as caves. Those footprints might be covered with rocks, but there could be places underneath big enough to hide in. This could be a possible hiding place."

"Do you think this is the kind of place where Vlad would really choose to hide?" Sebastian asked.

Chris was getting rather used to this young man asking important questions in a respectful way, and he liked it. He never wanted to turn into one of those monarchs who started thinking he was always right because nobody was ever brave enough to question him. With a wife like Marigold, the chances of that happening were dim, he admitted, but he didn't mind having someone else question him, too.

"Well, the trail stops here," Chris said. "But that could be just because I can't read it well on the rocks. I'm guessing, however, they're as tired of running as we are, and they're carrying Poppy, too. So it seems logical that they'd at least consider stopping here, though you're right, it definitely wouldn't be Vlad's first choice. So let's have a look, all right?"

"Yes, sire. That is completely cogitable." Sebastian was very pleased to be getting such an inside look at how sensibly and logically the king's mind worked. It was giving him a great feeling of confidence in his monarch, and also causing him to like Christian quite a bit.

Cogitable, thought Phoebe. *Wow.*

Down in their hole, Emlyn and Fogarty could hear voices. Once the voices stopped, they heard footsteps coming across the rocks, sliding and stumbling, but coming closer. Emlyn put her hand over Fogarty's mouth, just in case. Fogarty could be a little unpredictable. However much they wanted to be rescued, they needed to know who was out there before they revealed themselves. After all, these woods were full of rogues and brigands—rather like themselves, in fact—and being discovered might be worse than the fix they were already in.

Phoebe, perhaps because she was shortest and therefore closest to the ground, was the one who spotted the hole. Just in case there was someone down there, she didn't want to be obvious about it, so while she was yanking on Sebastian's sleeve and pointing at the opening, she was saying loudly, "This is a waste of time. Nobody could be hiding in this mess. It really is just a giant's playground."

Sebastian waved his arm to attract the king's attention. At the same time, he was answering Phoebe. "I agree. I don't think there's any place big enough to hide in there. Your Highness, I think we should move on."

Down below, Emlyn heard "Your Highness" and held her breath. Fogarty squeezed his eyes shut and crossed his fingers but couldn't help making a muffled sound.

13

UP ABOVE, SEBASTIAN AND Phoebe heard that sound. Phoebe jumped up and down a couple of times, pointing hard at the hole. Christian and Rollo, too, raised their eyebrows and cocked their heads in question. Sebastian nodded emphatically and mouthed, "They're down there."

Chris pulled Sebastian out of earshot of the hole while Rollo kept an eye on it. "Are you sure?" he whispered.

"Both Phoebe and I heard something. I suppose it could be some sort of animal. But if that was the case, I think we'd have heard more than just that one sound."

"Good thinking," Chris said, patting Sebastian's

shoulder. "I wonder if they're armed. Or if there's another way out of there."

"If there was another way out, I think they'd have taken it," Sebastian said. He was becoming less and less hesitant about giving his straight opinion to his king. In fact, he was forgetting that Chris *was* his king. "As for weapons, I don't know. But they did leave the lodge in a big hurry. Maybe too fast to grab anything."

"Let's hope so," Chris said. "Because we're going to have to get them out. Which may involve going in after them."

"Yes, I agree," Sebastian said.

"First we'll have to move some rocks to make the hole bigger. But we'll have to be careful, just in case there are weapons. As soon as we start moving rocks, they'll know we're on to them."

"We'll have to be fast," Sebastian said.

Chris nodded. "We can be. Let's get started."

The four of them hauled a few big rocks away, allowing cool spring light to pour down into the hole. Then they stood back, waiting to see if any sort of missile came flying out.

None did, since Emlyn had unwisely thrown out all the rocks that had been at the bottom of the hole.

It was at this point that Chris realized he wasn't sure what they would do if they got the kidnappers out. He assumed there were four, two of whom were the nastiest, scariest, most devious brutes the kingdom had ever seen. He had his halberd, Rollo had his battle ax, and Sebastian had his mace, but Phoebe had nothing. Having left two guards at the dragon's lair and sent one back to the castle, he feared the search party was now seriously outnumbered and underprepared.

Cautiously, Chris peered into the hole. All he saw were two pairs of feet. Two? Where were the others? Where was Poppy? What had they done with her? He could feel rage building up, but he worked to suppress it, knowing that a hot head is not often a wise head.

He brandished his halberd over the hole and yelled, "Who's in there? Are you too cowardly to answer?"

Apparently they were. The feet did not move.

"It appears there are only two people in there," Rollo said.

"Yes," Christian agreed. "But which two?"

"I'll bet you can guess," Sebastian said.

After a moment's consideration, Chris said, "You're right. Vlad and Boris would never allow themselves to be trapped in such a dead end. It's got to be the laundress and the other footman."

"Which means the Terrible Twos have escaped with your daughter," Sebastian said in a quiet voice. "They wouldn't have left her behind with the ransom still unpaid."

"Yes," the king said, equally solemnly. "And I would bet all two million ducats that these two have been cut out of their share."

"Knowing Vlad as I do, I'm afraid I have to agree with you."

Chris took a deep breath. "Well, even if they have been betrayed, they surely know something. So we must take some time to think about how to get them out of there. They're down too deep for us to reach them."

"And I believe it would be beyond foolish for anyone to try to go in after them. Only one person at a time could fit and that person would be way too vulnerable while he did it."

"We might as well get some rest," Chris said to Rollo, Phoebe, and Sebastian. "We need to come up with a plan for what to do next. They aren't going anywhere, and we have no idea where Vlad and Boris have gone." He stopped talking before the quaver he could feel behind his words became obvious. Then he sat down with his back against a sun-warmed rock and closed his eyes.

Rollo kept watch over the hole. Phoebe and Sebastian seated themselves while Phoebe rolled the wonderful word *egregious* around in her mind.

Speaking softly, so as to not disturb Chris or let Rollo hear, Phoebe said, "What would you do if you knew it was your father down there?"

Sebastian took a long time to answer. Finally he said, "I would wish we could just leave him there. Seal up that opening and leave him there."

"Me, too," Phoebe whispered. "If it was my father. But it makes me ashamed to think that. It's something he would do without a qualm, and I don't want to have a single thought that's anything like one that he would have." She felt tears come to her eyes, then fought them back.

After another long pause, Sebastian said, "We all get mad and think crazy, cruel thoughts sometimes. But to *act* on them is what's barbarous. Only a few do that. Like the Terrible Twos. That's what makes them terrible."

"You said *barbarous*," Phoebe said in admiration.

"Something wrong with *barbarous*?"

"No. Nothing. That's what's so great. It's the perfect word. Hardly anybody can do that, get just the perfect word. You do it all the time. The king's not bad at it, either—after all, he said *egregious*—but you're better. I've been noticing."

Suddenly Sebastian felt too self-conscious about his vocabulary to say anything at all.

And as usual, when Phoebe herself felt self-conscious, she spouted an odd fact. "Did you know that a hummingbird can beat its wings seventy times in one second?"

"No," Sebastian said. "I didn't know that."

After that they were both silent, keeping an eye on the hole. And on each other.

After what seemed a very long time, when the sun was past the zenith in the western sky and the afternoon air was cooling, Sebastian and Phoebe got to their feet and went to stand next to Christian, who still rested against the rock, his eyes closed. Sebastian cleared his throat loudly.

Chris opened his eyes and blinked a few times. "Yes, Sebastian? Phoebe? What is it?"

"I think Phoebe and I have come up with a way to get them out of there without anybody getting hurt," Sebastian said.

"And I've got a few ideas myself." Chris sat up straighter. "Let's hear yours."

"First, we roll some of these rocks down into the hole. Big rocks. Just a little smaller than the diameter of the hole."

Chris's expression brightened. "I see where you're going with this. Then what? I'm thinking fire myself."

"Yes, sire. That's what I was thinking, too."

"And then vines," Phoebe said. "From those trees right over there." She pointed.

Christian jumped to his feet. "Brilliant!"

Once all the rocks were collected, Chris yelled down into the hole, "Look out below if you don't want to get hit by a rock! There are a lot of them coming down!"

On Sebastian's signal, they began pushing the rocks into the hole, one after another. When the final stone had been pushed in, Chris, Sebastian, Rollo, and Phoebe stood coughing in the dust that had been stirred up.

"I think that's enough to do the trick," Sebastian said. "Now the fire."

Phoebe had gathered a pile of dried moss and twigs next to the hole, and she watched as Chris took a flint and steel from his knapsack. Those were things no experienced woodsman ever went into the forest without. As Chris stood over the little pile, struggling to strike a spark big enough to ignite it, he muttered, "I wish somebody would hurry up and invent matches. This is really tedious."

Finally a spark fell into the dried moss and a wisp of smoke rose from it. Gently, coaxingly, Chris, Sebastian, Phoebe, and Rollo blew on the tiny spark until the whole pile caught and became a merry little blaze with lots of smoke.

"Perfect!" Phoebe exclaimed, clapping her hands.

"Well done, sire," Sebastian said.

"Not bad, if I do say so myself," Chris said. "Now we need more tinder."

Bit by bit they added fuel until the fire was so big, they wished they had some marshmallows. Then Rollo took his battle ax and used it to push a burning section down the hole.

"Hey!" Emlyn yelled. "What are you trying to do, burn us alive?"

"Finally," Chris said. "A reaction."

"No!" Sebastian yelled into the hole. "We just want you out of there! The smoke is encouragement. If you pile up the rocks, you can climb out." Rollo pushed another burning section into the hole.

"As the smoke gets worse in there, you'll probably have to," Phoebe called. "We can wait!"

It didn't take long before they could hear a commotion, though the smoke made it impossible to see what was going on. Suddenly, through the billows, out popped Emlyn.

"None of this was my idea!" she shrieked. "I'm a victim myself! They threatened me with terrible things if I didn't cooperate!"

As her feet reached solid ground, she tried to run, but Rollo and Sebastian grabbed her before she could get anywhere. Phoebe was quick with the vines, and they had Emlyn tied up before she was quite sure what had happened. But that didn't shut her up.

"I was just a happy laundress!" she exclaimed. "Minding my own business. I'd never even met them, the Terrible Twos. Especially that time Fogarty and I got lost in the forest, looking for a private place to . . . I mean, to have a picnic. I never even knew we were so close to where they lived, out past the dragon. And nobody ever mentioned there could be so much money involved in a kidnapping. What would I want with all that money? I was a happy laundress."

"Is there any way to muzzle her?" Phoebe asked. "I can't stand all these excuses."

Chris delved into his knapsack and brought out a clean diaper, which he'd brought figuring Poppy would need it by the time they found her. He took pleasure in jamming it into Emlyn's mouth, cutting off her stream of pleas and denials.

"I hope you've got another one of those," Rollo said as Fogarty emerged, coughing and bellowing, "She's the one got me into all this! I was proud of my position as a footman in the castle. I had no interest in any kidnapping! None! She made me!" Muffled howls came from Emlyn as Phoebe and Rollo trussed Fogarty with the vines and gagged him with another diaper.

Christian picked his halberd up from the ground and ran his thumb along the very sharp edge of the blade. "Which one of you wants to tell me where Vlad and Boris have gone with my daughter?" he asked calmly.

Emlyn's eyes got very big and she shook her head wildly. Her hair, which had long since come undone from its bun, flopped back and forth across her face while she grunted noises, presumably of denial.

Fogarty shook his head, too, squealing in fear.

"You mean neither of you knows where they've gone?" Chris asked.

They continued shaking their heads and moaning.

"Then I guess it's back to the castle and the dungeons for the two of you," Chris said. "I'd hoped I wouldn't have to do that."

He really had hoped that. He'd hoped they would tell him where the villains and his baby were, so that he, Sebastian, and Rollo with their weapons—and Phoebe with her wits—could go right there and foil the kidnapping. Now things were much more difficult and complicated.

"May I suggest something, sire?" Sebastian asked.

"Of course," Chris said. "I've come to believe in your sound judgment and good ideas."

Well, that was about the nicest thing anybody had ever said to Sebastian, and it made him terribly afraid to say anything more. What if this was one time his judgment wasn't sound at all and his ideas were dreadful? But his king was waiting for him to speak, so he had to.

"I think it would work best if you and Rollo took the prisoners back to the castle and Phoebe and I went in search of our fathers. We know them better than anybody does, so we have the best chance of tracking them down."

"You're amateurs!" Rollo exclaimed, his professional pride hurt.

"And Poppy's *my* daughter," Chris said.

"We know," Phoebe said. "And no one knows better

than we do that the worst place for a little baby to be is with our fathers. We want to get her away from them as much as you do."

"We can't leave the prisoners unattended while we all go off searching," Sebastian said reasonably. "They could get loose. And we can't bring them with us. That would slow us down. Someone has to take them back." He stopped there. Unlike most people, he knew when to quit talking. He had made his case and understood that the person who had heard it now needed time to think it over.

After a moment, Christian's shoulders slumped and he said, "You're right. We'll take these vermin back to the castle and then we'll come right back here with your horses and be ready for you when you come back with the other vermin. Oh. Sorry. I know they're your fathers."

"It's okay," Sebastian said. "They *are* vermin."

"Indeed," Phoebe added.

"We'll hurry, but I can't promise we can get back before it's completely dark. How do you feel about being out here in the dark, searching?'

"I don't think we have a choice," Sebastian said.

"We're running out of time. We have to use every minute."

"Then, here." The king handed Sebastian his knapsack. "Take this. There's some food and water and some things for Poppy if—I mean *when*—you find her."

Sebastian took the knapsack. He and Phoebe had their own, too, of course, but he understood the king's need to help. And maybe they would be gone so long, they would need more supplies. Expecting to find Vlad and Boris by nightfall seemed wildly optimistic. "Thank you, Your Majesty. You can count on us."

He hoped he was right.

14

SEBASTIAN AND PHOEBE WATCHED as their king marched Emlyn and Fogarty off at the end of his halberd, back toward where the horses waited. Once the sound of their footsteps had faded into the trees, Phoebe said, "What do we do now? I have absolutely no idea where my father could be. Do you?"

"I've been giving it some thought," Sebastian said. "And I do have an idea. They still want the ransom, don't they? And that means they intend to go to the dragon's lair at sunset tomorrow. So they have to stay close enough to get there by then. We could just wait for them there."

"But the princess," Phoebe reminded him. "They

didn't take the goat; they're not even bothering to feed Poppy now. They might show up for the money and not have a baby to exchange for it. You know they'd just take the money and run again. And they have time now to make a better plan for escape. For all I know, they've made a deal with the flying monkeys."

"That would be bad, of course. But those monkeys are unusually hard to locate. I think they're going to try to use the dragon. They're fascinated by her, they want the ransom exchange made near her lair, and she could easily hold back an army with her flames, giving them plenty of time to get away."

"So where do you think they are now?"

"I may be wrong, but I think they've gone back to either Vlad's lodge or Boris's pigsty to wait it out. Those are the last places they'd expect anyone to look, since they've already been searched. And I think my father meant to leave your father behind in that hole, too, with Emlyn and Fogarty, but something went wrong."

"You think your father wants to be the Terrible One?"

"He's a loner, he's arrogant—thinks he's smarter than everybody, always has—and I'm sure he doesn't want to share the ransom money."

"My father may not be as smart as yours, but he's very tenacious. It's always been almost impossible to get him to stop something once he has his teeth into it, so to speak. Though sometimes, literally. Vlad is going to have a hard time getting rid of him, if that's his plan. And the dragon—what makes you think she'd cooperate with them?"

"She's a dragon, isn't she?" Sebastian said. "Since when do dragons have any scruples?"

Phoebe straightened her back, fire flashing in her eyes. "And just how many dragons have you known?"

"Well, only the one. But I've been hearing stories about them all my life."

"The same way people have heard stories about us?" she asked, her voice tight. "Just because of who our fathers are? Without any evidence of any kind that we've ever done anything the slightest bit wrong?"

Sebastian finally took a good look at her set face and blinked. "Oh," he said. After a silence, during which Phoebe continued to glare at him, he said, "I see your point. I'm sorry. That was very foolish of me. Wouldn't it be interesting if the dragon's not as big a threat as we think she is? But I don't think we should count on that.

Remember how much burning and scaring she's done over the years."

"I haven't forgotten that. But I don't want you to forget how easy it is to make judgments that are not based on any facts."

He took her hand. "Forgive me. Please." The look he gave her was so remorseful that she had no choice but to accede.

They stayed that way, gazing into each other's eyes for several long moments, until Phoebe cleared her throat and said, "Shouldn't we start looking for the Terrible Twos?"

Sebastian seemed to wake from a minor trance. "Yes. Yes, we certainly should."

"And if we find them, we should concentrate on saving Poppy, don't you think? Once we have her, the emergency is over. We can leave the Terrible Twos to Rollo and the guards."

"Exactly," Sebastian said, relieved.

"We know they're not feeding her, so we might hear her crying from hunger unless they're keeping her quiet somehow. Your father is well-known for his sleeping powders as well as for his poisons, isn't he?"

"Well, yes, but his sleeping powders are intended to put people to sleep permanently."

"Then, we better get going. Did the king tell you where the guards found Boris's place?"

"Enough that I'm pretty sure I can find it."

"Well, what are we waiting for?"

Pausing only long enough to divide the contents of Chris's knapsack into their own two, they set off.

By the time they located Boris's dwelling, it was almost full dark. Boris's lodge wasn't very far from Vlad's, but it was so concealed by overgrown vegetation that it was almost impossible to see. In fact, they would have missed it entirely if they hadn't spotted a glimmer of lantern light through the wild growth.

Phoebe grabbed Sebastian's arm and pointed. He appreciated the feeling of her hand on his bicep for an instant before he nodded. Both were wondering if the other was as fearful at the prospect of seeing the father they had never wanted anything more to do with.

"We should reconnoiter," Sebastian said.

"Yes," Phoebe said. "I suppose we should. What a lovely word. What does it mean?"

"Oh. Sorry. It means to look around. Check things out. Get the lay of the land."

"Definitely. But it's so dark."

"We'll have to be very sneaky. The only way we'll have any clue is to get close enough to look in a window. Do you think your father would have any booby traps?"

"I never knew him to be that organized, as you can probably tell by the mess outside here. He liked inventing new instruments of torture but he'd never clean up the clutter left over. He'd just push it aside and step over it. I guess that's a booby trap in itself."

Sebastian was offended by such appalling habits. But also relieved, under the circumstances. After a long hesitation, he said, "So we should go. Have a look."

"I know we have to. But I'm scared. Are you?"

He smiled down at her. "Why should I be afraid of one of the nastiest, scariest, most devious brutes the kingdom has ever known? Sure, I'm scared. I've always been afraid of my father. I should be. *Everybody* should be. But do we have a choice? We promised the king we'd rescue Poppy."

Phoebe took a deep breath. "You're right. Thank

you for reminding me." She began pushing through the tangle of undergrowth toward Boris's house, and Sebastian followed.

They eased toward the window, trying not to make much noise, and arranged themselves on either side of it. When Sebastian nodded, Phoebe bobbed up and darted a look inside, then nodded at Sebastian, who darted his own look. They crouched beneath the window to compare notes.

"Did you see the baby?" Phoebe asked.

"I saw the laundry basket with the royal seal that they took her away in. But it was covered with a towel. I'm not sure she was in there."

"Of course she's in there. Why else would they have the basket?"

"But the Terrible Twos are surely there, too. How will we get Poppy?"

"We need a distraction. Something that will get them out so we can grab the laundry basket."

"A distraction," Sebastian murmured. "Like a lot of noise?"

"Maybe not that," she said. "If you were in an isolated house in the middle of the forest and you heard a strange sound outside, would *you* go running out to see what it was? Or would you stay inside where it was safe?"

"So we have to make it seem unsafe in there. I know! We could set the place on fire. Then they'd have to come out."

Phoebe considered this. "I'd be afraid of starting a forest fire. I couldn't bear that."

And he couldn't bear the stricken look in her eyes. "All right. Well, we could break some windows. That should alarm them."

"But enough to come out and see what caused it? Or enough to make them hole up inside even tighter?"

"Hmmm. Hard to know. Well, I guess there's only one thing to do."

"What?"

"We knock on the door and when they open it, hope they're surprised enough that we can rush in, grab the laundry basket, and rush out again."

"Wow. That's pretty daring. But maybe direct, straightforward action *is* the best thing."

"Come on, then." He took her hand and began pulling her toward the front door.

"Oh! You mean now?" She dug in her heels.

"How will it get better if we wait? We'll just get colder and more scared."

They tiptoed up the front steps, which were littered with leaves and other trash, and raised the door knocker, which, to Phoebe, looked like a leftover part from one of Boris's torture devices. Sebastian took a tender look at her and let the knocker fall.

Faster than they had anticipated, they heard heavy footsteps approaching the door, which was flung open to reveal Boris. He was so large, he filled the entire doorway, dashing their plan to rush past and grab the laundry basket.

"Phoebe?" Boris said. "What are you doing here?"

"Well, I, uh, I . . ."

"Have you come to your senses and decided to join your old dad after all?"

The elation in his voice made Phoebe pause. Maybe he really had missed her. Maybe even one of the nastiest, scariest, most devious brutes the kingdom had ever known could have a soft spot for his little girl. Or maybe, her realistic side reminded her, his motivation was something entirely more selfish, nasty, and/or devious. Yes, she had to admit, probably that.

"Come in, come in." He opened the door wider. "And you, too. Sebastian, isn't it?"

Phoebe and Sebastian threw each other a what-do-we-do-now look, then stepped inside. Almost before they could register the extent of the disarray in the room—pigsty, indeed!—Vlad stepped out from behind the door and blew a handful of sleeping powder from the palm of his hand into their faces.

Their last vision, before they fell to the floor, sound asleep, was of Vlad's evil and very satisfied smile. And the last thing they heard was Boris saying, "I'll throw them in the storeroom. They'll never get out of there."

15

A PLACE WITHOUT WINDOWS IN the middle of the night is about as dark as it gets, as Phoebe and Sebastian discovered when they woke up. They said each other's names, using the sound to locate each other, the way bats do. When they finally did, they clung together like lost souls, which is exactly how they were feeling.

"The door's locked," Sebastian said. "I already tried it. And as you've found out, there's plenty of stuff in here to trip over, so we have to be careful."

"You're still wearing your knapsack!" Phoebe exclaimed as she hugged him. "And so am I! We can use the flint and steel and make a fire for some light!"

He slid the straps off his shoulders. "If we can find

them by feel. And if we can find something that will burn."

"Are you sounding discouraged?" Phoebe asked. "Don't! We're still kicking and we have tools to help ourselves. Think! What is in your knapsack that might burn? What's in mine?"

"Um, let's see. Crackers. Diapers. A handkerchief. Clean socks. My Arthurian mace . . ."

"Oh! Oh!" Phoebe exclaimed. "I've got the king's map! The one we transferred from his knapsack! We're beyond needing a map by now. Let's make a fire with it and get a look at what else is in here. Maybe there'll be something we can use to get ourselves out."

Sebastian could hear her rummaging through her knapsack, so he did the same. After quite a bit more rummaging, a lot of trial and error, and a couple of bad words, they managed to locate the flint and steel, get a spark, and set the map afire. It is amazing what something as simple and as magical as light can do to improve one's spirits. Phoebe and Sebastian danced around the merry little blaze as if they were the first to invent fire.

"Quick now," Sebastian said. "We have to find more

to burn so we can keep our fire going. And then we have to go through all this"—he flung out his arms, indicating the heaps of junk strewn around the room—"to see what we can find that will help us."

They soon accumulated enough scraps of wood and paper, as well as a few oily rags, to assure themselves illumination for quite a while.

"I wish I knew how long we were asleep," Phoebe said as she picked through debris. "Is it still night, so maybe the Terrible Twos are sleeping? Or is it daytime again and they're waiting out there to do something worse to us? Or does it not matter at all, because they're just going to abandon us here to molder away?"

"Thank you," Sebastian said grimly. "I needed cheering up."

"Oh. Sorry," she said, abashed. "I was just thinking out loud." To make up for her thoughtlessness, she asked, "Did you know that nine out of ten people struck by lightning are hit in the afternoon?"

He couldn't help smiling. "No. I didn't know that. We must stay inside every rainy afternoon. *If* we ever get out of here."

"Look!" she said, lifting something from a pile. "A key!"

He took it from her and examined it. "Don't get your hopes up. Chances are it won't fit this lock."

Sebastian was right. He worked at it for many long minutes, but no matter how he twisted and turned it, the key wouldn't open the door. Frustrated, he threw it back into the heap of trash, then sank to the floor, his head in his hands. King Arthur would never have felt such despair. Phoebe was right. They probably would molder away in here.

She had come to stand over him, wringing her hands. "Did you know that most people have one foot bigger than the other?" she asked uncertainly. "And that it's usually the left? Are you all right?"

He shook his head. "It's looking like we will never escape. And I think my right foot is bigger. That's what the boot maker says."

"Oh, well, there are always exceptions, of course. Don't be so hard on yourself. We're not finished yet."

She was right. Surely King Arthur wouldn't give up so quickly. Certainly not. Sebastian got to his feet. "Do you want to look for another key while I try to find something else that might help us?"

"Sure," Phoebe said, relieved to see him up and at it again, though not so excited at the prospect of digging through the debris in the storeroom again. She went back to the pile and began sorting, glad that mostly she had no idea what the rubble had been used for.

Sebastian chose his own pile to explore, tossing things aside as he made his way to the bottom. "Hey!" he said, holding something up. "I've found a rasp. I'm not even going to speculate about how Boris used it, but I might be able to do something with it."

Phoebe was sorting through a bunch of tattered shirts when she felt something in one of the pockets. "Look!" she exclaimed. "Here's another key!"

It didn't open the door, either, but Sebastian said, "Let me tackle it for a while. Maybe I can modify it with this rasp and get it to work."

It was a pleasure for Phoebe to watch Sebastian's intent face as he scraped away on the prongs of the key. Watching the play of the firelight on the muscles in his forearm wasn't so bad, either.

"Well, let's try it," he finally said, inserting the key

into the lock. He twiddled with it for a few minutes and then withdrew it. "I can feel I've almost got it. It needs just a little bit of adjustment."

After a few more passes with the rasp, he again put the key into the lock and very delicately manipulated it until there was a solid click.

"Did you do it?" Phoebe whispered, her hands clenched on her chest.

"I think so. But now we *really* have to be quiet." Gingerly he removed the key, stuck it in his pocket, and tried the door handle. It moved. It turned. The door came open a crack.

"Ooh," Phoebe breathed, and Sebastian put a finger against her lips to hush her. She didn't mind at all.

Sebastian opened the door wider, inch by inch, until he could look out. "It's still night," he whispered right into Phoebe's ear. "And it's very quiet out there. Maybe they're asleep."

They put on their knapsacks and he took her hand, leading her into a dark hallway. They tiptoed along the hall toward a faint glow, carefully avoiding unidentified strewn objects. The hallway opened into the large room they'd had only a glimpse of earlier, before they'd been knocked out. Boris lay sprawled on a long table, snoring away, a candle burning on a bench beside him.

In a far dark corner, sitting upright, was Vlad. They would have missed seeing him if they hadn't been searching for him. And at his feet was the laundry basket.

Phoebe and Sebastian stood paralyzed, barely breathing, their hearts sinking. After several immobile moments, Sebastian put his lips to Phoebe's ear and whispered, "He hasn't moved. I think he's asleep."

"Sitting straight up like that?"

"I've seen him do it lots of times. I've been watching for a gleam from his eyes, but I haven't seen one. So they must be closed. I'll get the baby. You get the door open so we can run. He can wake up and be fully alert in an instant. I've seen that lots of times, too."

Phoebe felt faint and dizzy, but knew she had to force herself to get silently across the room and get the door open somehow. She *had* to. She took a breath so deep it made her see stars for a moment, and then ventured out, pausing to catch her breath after every step, her eyes never leaving Vlad's sleeping figure.

Sebastian crept closer and closer to Vlad. He had always been afraid of his father, but never so much as now. The fact that Sebastian was his very own son would make no difference at all to Vlad when it came to exacting vengeance for disloyalty.

A floorboard creaked beneath Sebastian's foot. Fortunately it coincided with one of Boris's snores, which disguised the sound.

Sweat had beaded on Sebastian's forehead and begun to run into his eyes by the time he reached Vlad's chair. He stood for a moment, assuring himself that Vlad's eyes were indeed closed. He had his hands on the laundry basket, ready to lift, when he noticed a string fastened to it. He followed the string until he saw that it was tied around Vlad's ankle. Sebastian wiped the sweat from his eyes with his sleeve and worked at unknotting the string on the laundry basket. Once it was undone, he checked all around for more booby traps, then looked back at Phoebe and nodded.

Phoebe took hold of the cold handle and pulled—and nothing happened. Desperate, she yanked on it again, but it still didn't budge. She could see Sebastian coming toward her, his eyes wide, the laundry basket in his arms. Her mind was blank. Finally she thought, *Lock. There must be a lock.*

She fumbled around the handle until she found a little knob. It made a small *snick* sound as she turned it, and then the door edged open. All the blood seemed to leave her head, and she was afraid she would faint. She had time for only a couple of deep breaths before Sebastian was right there. He pushed the door farther open with his foot and they were out.

"Run!" he whispered hoarsely.

16

PHOEBE AND SEBASTIAN HURRIED down the filthy steps, pushed through the tangled growth around the house, and took off through the trees. They could see the beginnings of dawn in the sky above the trees, and the birds were starting their sunrise songs.

Strong as Sebastian was, he couldn't run forever carrying a basket full of baby. "I have to stop for a minute," he gasped. "Besides, we should take a look at the princess. See if she's all right."

Phoebe wasn't happy about stopping—she wanted to be much farther from Boris and Vlad—but she, too, needed to catch her breath.

Sebastian set the basket down and pulled the towel off. Inside lay a pale and limp baby, barely breathing.

"Oh, my," Phoebe said. "Do you suppose Vlad used the sleeping powder on her?"

"I'm sure of it," Sebastian said, jiggling the basket gently to try to wake Poppy up. "I'm just not sure if he knew the right dose for somebody so little. She's awfully still. And she hasn't had any milk for a long time."

"Then we have to get her back to the castle fast!"

But before they could make a move, crashing noises came through the forest. The way sound bounced through the trees, they couldn't tell if the commotion was behind them or ahead of them.

"The Terrible Twos?" Phoebe whispered. "We have to hide!"

Desperately they looked around, but there were no convenient caves, or hollow logs, or piles of rocks to hide behind. Then through the trees came Christian, Rollo, and a troop of castle guards, all on horseback and leading two riderless horses.

Once again Phoebe thought she might faint, but she

was getting pretty good at taking deep breaths and remaining on her feet. "Oh, Your Highness, are we glad to see you!" she called.

"Likewise," Chris said, leaping off his horse and rushing toward the laundry basket. He snatched up the baby and clutched her to his chest, suppressing a sob. Poppy drooped limply in his arms. "She's breathing," he said with relief. "I brought the court doctor with me, just in case." He turned and called to the doctor, then put Poppy back into the basket and handed it to him. "Do whatever it takes, but keep her alive!"

"Of course, Your Majesty." The doctor bent over the basket, thinking about what ex-queen Olympia and the Terrible Twos would have done to him if he had been unsuccessful at something they had requested. He was pretty sure King Christian was more enlightened, but he didn't want to take any chances. He was going to take *very* good care of this little patient.

Christian turned his attention to Phoebe and Sebastian. "We'd have gotten here sooner but it took longer for us to get back to the castle in the darkness than I thought it would. And then we had to get organized, and . . ."

"It's okay," Sebastian said. "We only just got here."

"Where are they?" The king's eyes were narrow and his jaw was set.

"If you hurry, you might be able to catch them still asleep. We left them back that way, at Boris's place."

Chris sprang onto his horse. "Wait here. We'll be back for you." He raised his arm, cried, "Follow me!" to Rollo and his troops, and they all charged off into the forest.

Phoebe sank onto the ground and leaned against a tree. She had finally run out of gas. Sebastian joined her. They didn't have to say a word. They each knew what the other was thinking: *Thank goodness Chris, Rollo, and the guards had shown up when they did!*

After a moment, Phoebe said, "We left the fire burning in the storeroom."

"Don't worry," Sebastian assured her. "It'll burn itself out on that stone floor without more fuel. It won't burn Boris's house down, though that probably would be the most efficient way to clean up that mess."

"But without the mess, we wouldn't have gotten out of there. So sometimes even a mess is a good thing."

Sebastian smiled fondly at her. *Seeing the rosy side of any situation is quite a nice quality to have,* he thought. He reached out and took her hand, and together they watched the court physician work over Poppy.

Quite a while passed before they heard horses approaching once again. They got to their feet as Chris and the castle guards rode through the trees, flanking two horses carrying Vlad and Boris, whose hands were tied behind their backs.

"Phoebe!" Boris yelled. "Phoebe, is that you? Help me, Phoebe. I'm innocent. I had nothing to do with any kidnapping. I was just minding my own business in my own house. I'm harmless. You know that. Tell them. Tell them!"

Phoebe turned her back on him. "You've never, ever been harmless," she said. "That's all I have to say."

Boris's pitiful imploring was over. "You ungrateful brat!" he yelled. "Who devoted himself to you after your mother abandoned you? Who sacrificed to make sure you had everything you needed? Who made you your own little guillotine for your birthday? It's your duty to help me now!"

Phoebe kept her back turned and pressed her lips tightly together to keep from sobbing. What little girl wants a guillotine for her birthday? He didn't even build it for her, anyway. It was a scale model for a full-sized one he was constructing. What he gave her was essentially a leftover. He had never sacrificed a single thing for her.

She felt a warm hand take hers. Sebastian gave her hand a gentle squeeze but said nothing. He didn't have to. She tried to think if anything had ever felt as good to her as that warm hand on hers. Aside from one or two vague memories of her mother's hugs, the answer was *no*.

She squeezed his hand back. She knew his own father was just as mean and twice as smart as Boris.

Boris continued yelling invective at Phoebe until Rollo poked him in the stomach with his lance. But that wasn't enough to shut him up entirely.

"Vlad! Vlad!" Boris hollered. "Tell them this is all a big mistake. Tell them, Vlad!"

But Vlad maintained a haughty silence, as if he couldn't lower himself far enough to communicate with such rabble. Sebastian knew that meant his mind was working a mile a minute, which was a scary thing to contemplate. It was a big mistake to ever assume that Vlad was under anybody's control.

Phoebe could see that Sebastian was upset and worried, and as usual, she couldn't think of the right thing to say about that. So she said, "Did you know that grasshoppers are three times as nutritious as beefsteak?"

Sebastian refocused on her. "No, I didn't. But at this moment, I'd settle for either. Are you as hungry as I am?"

"I hadn't thought about it until you mentioned it, but now I'm ravenous. I have apples in my knapsack. And some cheese. Would you like some?"

He nodded. "And I have crackers."

Boris continued bellowing his innocence and his outrage, Vlad maintained an icy silence, and Christian conferred with the doctor about Poppy.

Eventually Chris said, "We need to start back. I

want to get these miscreants into the dungeon as fast as I can. But let them walk. Phoebe and Sebastian deserve the horses."

Miscreants, Phoebe thought. *Perfect.*

Tenderly Chris picked up the laundry basket. "I'll carry this," he said.

17

Phoebe couldn't see Vlad and Boris behind her, but she could hear her father grumbling and cursing and stumbling as they went. In spite of this racket, she began to doze as her horse plodded along. After all, it had been a long, strange, difficult night.

So she missed seeing the flames that leaped above the treetops ahead of them. What woke her was Sebastian's voice saying, "There's the dragon. And she seems to still be upset about something, judging from those flames."

"We're going to the lair while Rollo and his guards take the Terrible Twos back to the castle dungeon.

Now that we have Poppy, I'm not going back without my Marigold," Chris said.

When the smaller party arrived at the clearing in front of the lair, they found the dragon there, belching blasts of flame while the two guards who had been left to try to rescue Marigold cowered just out of reach of the conflagration. They both started talking at once when they saw the king.

"Your Highness! We tried, honestly . . ."

"Sire, it's not our fault the queen is still . . ."

"Please, Your Majesty. We're not fireproof . . ."

"Highness, that dragon seems to like having the queen there . . ."

Chris held up a hand to silence them after he noticed three women sitting on tree stumps, holding out sticks with weenies stuck on them for the dragon to roast . . . and one of the women was Queen Marigold.

"Marigold!" Christian shouted. He thrust the laundry basket at the court doctor and dismounted. "Are you all right?" He hesitated to rush directly to her, considering the unpredictability of the dragon's flame-shooting propensities.

Instead, Marigold dropped her stick and ran into his

arms. "Oh, Chris!" she cried. "I knew you'd come back for me. What about Poppy? Have you found her?"

"Yes. I have her. Are you all right? Have you been harmed?" He held her face in his hands and looked down into her eyes as if no one else even existed.

Phoebe looked on with awe and envy. No one had ever looked at her quite that way.

"No, no, I'm fine," Marigold said. "I could even have enjoyed myself if I hadn't been so worried about you and Poppy. Is she all right?"

"Yes." He didn't elaborate.

"Just *yes*?" Her voice wavered. "What aren't you telling me?"

"Doctor," Chris said, turning back. "Hand me down the basket." He had learned not to keep the truth from her, however distressing.

Marigold bent over the basket. "It *is* Poppy!" she cried, picking the baby up and looking down into her peaceful, unconscious face. "But what's wrong with her? Did they do something to her? Did they hurt her?" Her voice rose. "Where are they? Did you catch them?"

"I got them. They're on their way to the dungeon. But Poppy has been the victim of one of Vlad's sleeping potions." Chris refrained from telling her that the Terrible Twos hadn't bothered to keep feeding Poppy. There was such a thing as too much information—especially if the time when the information would have mattered was over. He could tell her later—much later—when the impact would, with luck, be less.

"I know this is awful to say," Marigold said, clutching Poppy close to her chest. "But right now I would like to do every single thing to them that they ever did to any of their victims."

"See?" Sebastian whispered to Phoebe. "Everybody thinks awful thoughts sometimes, even Queen Marigold. But only bad people actually do them. So she won't."

"We need to get back to the castle," Chris said. "I want to make sure those vermin are locked up tight, and I want the court doctor to make Poppy comfortable. And I want to get you away from this beast." He'd lowered his voice, just in case the dragon took offense in an incendiary way. "How hard will it be? The guards said the dragon wants to keep you here."

"Oh, you have that all wrong," Marigold said. "She's not a beast. Oh, well, yes, she is a beast. She's a dragon, after all. But she's not *bad*. She's just unhappy. And misunderstood. And she has a medical problem, too. But she took very good care of me. And she did like having me as a guest. And Anabel and Twyla, too."

"Who?"

"Them." Marigold pointed to the two women sitting in the shadows near the entrance to the lair, their weenie sticks dangling forgotten in their hands as they watched. "They've lived with her for a long time."

"Lived with the dragon? You mean, in the lair?" Chris's eyebrows had climbed up quite high on his forehead.

"I'm incredulous," Sebastian whispered to Phoebe. "So is the king."

Incredulous, thought Phoebe. *I'm incredulous that he used that wonderful word.*

"Yes," Marigold said. "They feel very safe in there. They'll all understand I have to leave now, but I do have to say goodbye." Still carrying Poppy, she went to Anabel and Twyla, showing them the sleeping baby before they hugged her goodbye.

Then, to everyone's surprise, Marigold did the same with the dragon, first showing her the baby and then draping her arm around the shimmering scaly neck. She pressed her forehead against the forehead of the dragon—who lowered her eyelashes in what could have been a bashful way—for a moment, before she went to join Christian.

Then the dragon blinked her long lashes in the direction of the waiting group and sent a series of white, heart-shaped puffs of smoke at them.

Uneasily they headed for home, the two singed guards bringing up the rear. Marigold held the baby and rode in front of Christian, who was happy to have them safe in his arms. But there was something he didn't understand.

"Marigold," he said. "I have to ask you something."

"Of course," she said. "Anything."

"If you insist that the dragon is simply unhappy and misunderstood, but not bad, why didn't you escape? It sounds like you could have just walked away."

"I was so desperate when I first ran in there, I wasn't thinking straight. But when I calmed down and saw that there was no danger, I realized that if I left, I would just make things worse by getting lost in the woods. You know I have no sense of direction. Then, when the guards showed up, I thought I could leave, but by then, Winnie was feeling very protective of me, the same way she feels about Twyla and Anabel, and didn't trust them to take good care of me. I know she was overreacting, but it's hard to argue with someone who keeps erupting. So I figured the smartest thing I could do was to wait for you to come back, after you'd found Poppy and caught the Terrible Twos. I know it was rash of me to rush into Winnie's lair, but I was nearly out of my mind about Poppy."

"Winnie?"

"The dragon."

Christian was touched by her confidence in him, at how certain she was that he could find Poppy, capture the Terrible Twos, and wrest her from the dragon. But he also worried. "Will you promise me that next time you'll think first before rushing off somewhere that seems dangerous? It worked out all right this time, but . . ."

"I know," Marigold said, abashed. "You're right. But

what do you mean *next time*? How many times do you think something like this is going to happen?"

He shrugged. "Maybe not just like this, but *something* will happen. That's just life. Something always happens. Sometimes good, sometimes not so good, but we need to have cool heads for whatever it is."

"I know that's good advice," she said. "But it's so hard to do."

"I know," he said. "But we have a whole kingdom to think about, not only ourselves and Poppy. We have to try harder than anyone, and be good examples."

Marigold considered how easy that was to forget, since she'd never expected to be a queen. But Chris had never expected to be a king, either. "You're a good example to me, too," she said. "Thank you."

Nobody ever gets enough appreciation, even kings, so it warmed Chris's heart to hear those words. "You inspire me to do my best," he said. "So I thank you, too."

They rode the rest of the way home grateful to be together once again.

* * *

Back at the castle, Marigold hustled off to the nursery with Poppy and the doctor, and Christian went to the dungeon.

"I want double guards down here all the time," Chris told Rollo. "They're staying put right here until the trial."

The king knew how eager a prisoner could be to escape. And how hard one could try to do so. And how it was not impossible.

With the excitement over for a while, Phoebe headed back to the library. She doubted anyone had tried to check out a book while she was gone, but she had left a note saying she'd get their books to them if they would leave their names and the titles on a slip of p-mail paper.

To her surprise, Sebastian tagged along. "Do you mind?" he asked. "I thought I'd get a book to help me fall asleep tonight. I'm a little too wound up to go to sleep easily."

Phoebe didn't like the idea of someone using a book as a sleeping pill, but she supposed she should be happy about anything that got someone reading. There was always the chance that he would like the book enough that it would keep him awake.

"Of course," she said, noting with disappointment that no requests for books waited at the door.

As always when she returned to the library, she felt as if she had come back to the only thing close to a home she had ever known. It was quiet, and safe, and pretty—something her childhood home never had been, what with her father always noisily building some ugly torture device. Or using it.

"It's nice in here," Sebastian said. "Quiet. Pretty." And after a long pause, he sighed and added, "Safe." Part of what made the place feel safe to him was her—her competence, her calmness, her radiance.

Phoebe stared at him. "I was just thinking that."

He gave a little nod and wandered over to the shelves, looking for his bedtime book, while Phoebe gazed after him. How was it possible, she wondered, that he shared any genes with Vlad?

18

Down in the dungeon, Vlad at last broke his silence. He waited until the two guards had wandered over by the stairs and were having a chat about the new upstairs chambermaid. Then he began rummaging through his pockets, pulling out little bits of this and that, things that didn't look like anything but lint or strips of p-mail paper or string or sand. He laid them all out on the bottom bunk in the cell he shared with Boris.

"What do you say we get out of here?" Vlad whispered.

"Yeah, right. Have you noticed we're behind bars? And that there are two guards over there carrying so many weapons, it's a surprise they can still stand up?"

"Not a problem." Vlad fiddled with his little pile of things.

"Right," said Boris again, and lay back on the upper bunk. "I'm beat. That was a long walk. We didn't even have a chance for that dragon to help us! You'd think she would be more friendly, considering I named a torture instrument after her—a very effective one, too, I have to say. And you named your best poison after her, too."

"I didn't expect her to help us. She's spurned every overture we ever made to her—usually with lots of fireworks, too. You were living in a dream world if you thought she would come to our aid. The only one you can really depend on is yourself," Vlad murmured as he continued fiddling. "It pays to always be prepared."

"Blah, blah, blah," Boris muttered, thinking what a know-it-all Vlad was. Thought he knew better than anybody about *everything*. Boris wished he'd insisted on separate cells, even if the guards thought they'd be easier to watch if they were locked up together the way Emlyn and Fogarty were. The guards over there in the corner, gossiping, weren't even watching, Boris noted.

Soon Boris was snoring, while Vlad continued with his project. So the kidnapping hadn't been a success, he thought. True, that was a disappointment, but not everything worked out the way one wanted it to. One had to be willing and able to roll with the punches, to survive to fight again another day. Naturally, it meant he would have to go far away, but he'd planned to do that, anyway—maybe just not as far away as would now be necessary. So there was no great loss—aside from all those ducats, of course. But there were opportunities elsewhere, other places where his talents would be appreciated, where there would be chances to make more ducats. The important thing was to escape. Until that happened, his possibilities were seriously limited.

Taking Boris with him wasn't ideal, but there were times when having a big, strong, rather dim brute with you could be useful. In his experience, a lot of women seemed to feel that way, too. Vlad hummed a little as he worked.

The afternoon passed into evening, and then into the dead of night.

In the deepest part of the night, Boris snored so

loudly he woke himself up. He turned over and peered down to see Vlad, outlined by the light from the wall torches, sitting peacefully on the floor, his back against the wall.

"Oh," Vlad said, getting to his feet. "You're awake. Just in time."

"Time for what?" Boris scrubbed his face with his hands, trying to wake up.

"Time to go," Vlad whispered.

"You're kidding, right?"

Vlad shook his head. "I'm going to blast the lock off this door, then I'm going to blow my sleeping powder on the guards. But you're going to stand by to bang their heads together, just in case the powder doesn't work fast enough. And then we're going out the disposal tunnel, where I'll blast out the door that opens onto the riverbank."

"Hey! I'd forgotten about that tunnel. They used to dump the torture victims through there, out into the river." Boris rubbed his hands together. "What are we waiting for?" He jumped off the upper bunk with enough of a crash that Vlad flinched.

"Quiet, you oaf!" he hissed. "We don't want to wake

those guards until we have to. And we don't want to wake up Emlyn and Fogarty, either. They're not coming with us."

That was fine with Boris. He'd never really liked either of them—probably because he didn't really like anybody—and trying to escape with four would be more than twice as hard as trying to escape with two.

They held still for a moment but heard nothing more than heavy, sleepy breathing coming from both guards and the prisoners in the other cell.

Vlad began packing something squishy around the lock in the cell door. He whispered, "Interestingly, this is the same stuff King Christian used to get out of the dungeon years back, in those crazy days before he married the princess. I learned the formula for it after I found out he'd used it. You never know when an odd bit of knowledge like that will come in handy."

"Yeah, yeah," Boris said. "Get on with it."

So Vlad did. And with a loud *pop!* the lock on the cell door blew off and the door swung open. The *pop!* was enough to wake the guards, who scrambled up and came running. As soon as they were in range, Vlad dipped a hand into his pocket and blew powder into their faces. The guards came to a sudden stop, rubbing their eyes. They probably would have fallen of their own accord, but Boris couldn't resist. It had been too long since he'd been able to do damage to anyone. He took their heads into his large, meaty hands, and banged them together. The impact made the sound of a bowling ball striking pins, and the guards went down in a heap. Boris thought he could almost see stars circling their heads, and he felt better than he had in a long time.

By that time, Emlyn and Fogarty were on their feet, standing at the door to their cell. "Hurry up!" Emlyn called. "Get our door open, too."

"Sorry," Vlad said, moving swiftly by. "Not this time."

"What do you mean, *this* time?" Fogarty asked. "There's not going to be any other time."

"Oh," said Vlad, halting for a moment. "You're right. So sorry. And goodbye."

"Hey!" yelled Emlyn. Fogarty joined her, but yelling was futile. Vlad and Boris had disappeared into the mouth of the disposal tunnel.

Emlyn and Fogarty yelled for a while longer, just on principle. Finally, Emlyn, whose throat was getting sore, flopped down on the lower bunk. "We should have known we couldn't trust them," she said. "After all, they did have the worst reputations in the kingdom."

"I feel like an idiot," Fogarty said. "And a dupe. And a failure."

"Well, you are!" Emlyn assured him. She didn't want to say that she was thinking the same thing about herself. She curled up, determined to go back to sleep. Might as well. All the excitement was over, and it hadn't included her.

Sebastian selected a book at random from the library shelf. What he'd really wanted was to spend a few more minutes with Phoebe, but that wasn't working out so well. He had thought he felt her gaze on him as he perused the stacks, but when he darted a peek in her direction, she was sitting at her desk paying no attention at all to him. He cleared his throat and she raised her head.

"I guess I'll take this one, then," he said, holding out a book.

"*Ancient Agrarian Practices*? Really? Well, it ought to

do the job of putting you to sleep." She wrote the title in her ledger and handed it back to him.

"Well. Good night, then," he said.

She avoided his eyes. What was the point? They'd shared an adventure that was now over. She would go back to being the daughter of Boris, the reviled torturer-in-chief, whose grisly reputation would now be resurrected just as it had begun to fade a little. And her own name would be unfavorably linked to his all over again.

"Good night," she said to Sebastian.

He had no choice but to leave, even though her voice had had a trace of something curious in it. Regret? Resignation? Loneliness?

Instead of going back to his cramped room over the blacksmith shop, Sebastian went up to the broad terrace that spanned the width of the castle and looked down over the river. A lot of dramatic things had occurred on that terrace, Sebastian thought as he leaned on the parapet. But to other people. Nothing was going to happen to him now. He would live out his life as an isolated blacksmith's assistant, entertaining himself by making faithful models of King Arthur's exploits, not having any adventures of his own.

Now that Vlad was back in the limelight, Sebastian was sure he would never escape the pall that his father's reputation continued to cast over him. This kidnapping episode would be merely a blip in his life—a blip connected to his father, just like everything always was.

Sighing, he gazed down at the river flowing past in the darkness. He could hear the gurgle of the water as it passed over rocks, and see the light from the security torches around the castle sparkling on the surface.

This idyllic view was interrupted by the sound of a blast. Sebastian leaned farther over the parapet to see what was happening. To his amazement, the flickering torchlight revealed his father, followed by Boris, tumbling out of a doorway in the castle wall and onto the riverbank. They stood there for a moment, apparently arguing, and then headed off along the river's edge toward the Zandelphia-Beaurivage Bridge.

19

THE TERRIBLE TWOS HAD escaped! They were loose again, ready to do more harm—if not in Zandelphia-Beaurivage, then in some other innocent kingdom. He should have known they'd find a way to get out, Sebastian thought. They never gave up.

But they had done enough damage. Sebastian braced his shoulders and vowed he would not allow that to continue.

He didn't want to wake the king. And if he went for Rollo and the guards, by the time he made the necessary explanations, the Terrible Twos would be well on their way. The only solution was to go after them now, on his own. He wasn't sure what he would do when he caught up with them, but he would think of something before it happened. He wasn't going to let those two ruin any more lives than they already had.

Sebastian tore down the winding staircase from the terrace, erupted into the passageway, and blasted out into the village square just in time to collide with Phoebe, on her way to her chambers after closing up the library. He grabbed her hand and pulled her along with him as he ran.

"Your father and mine have escaped! We have to stop them! They can't be allowed to wreak any more havoc!"

"*Wreak!*" she said, running along with him. "*Havoc!* What wonderful words! Wait—what? The Terrible Twos have escaped? What can *we* do about it? Shouldn't we get the guards?"

"It would take too much time. Vlad and Boris are probably already on the bridge. We can't let them get away!"

It was crazy, she knew it was, to think that the two of them could do anything about the Terrible Twos, but Sebastian seemed so determined, and so certain, that he was irresistible. She kept running.

They sped out of the village and tore to the Zandelphia-Beaurivage Bridge, just in time to see the Terrible Twos reach the other end.

"Watch which way they go," Sebastian panted. "We can still catch them. And we'll have the element of surprise. They don't know we're after them."

It helped that Phoebe and Sebastian were young and fit, and that Boris was fat and slow. Though Vlad had kept himself in good shape, he had already had a strenuous few days and he wasn't as young as he used to be, in spite of the concoctions he formulated to make himself feel younger. You can't really fool Mother Nature, no matter how hard you try.

The moonless night helped hide Phoebe and Sebastian, though it made keeping the escapees in sight more difficult. Fortunately, Boris made a lot of noise, crashing through the brush.

Soon Phoebe and Sebastian were close enough to hear Boris say, "We gotta stop. I'm all out of breath."

"Soon," Vlad said. "We're going to need some help, and I know where we're going to get it."

"What does he mean?" Phoebe whispered to Sebastian. "Who would help them?"

"I can't imagine," Sebastian replied. "The king and queen have rooted out all the troublemakers. And I haven't heard about any of them, except the Terrible Twos, staying in the vicinity."

Vicinity, Phoebe thought. He could have said *neighborhood* or *area,* but he said *vicinity.* "Did you know that nothing rhymes with *orange?*" she said. "Or with *purple, silver,* or *window?*"

"I didn't know that," he said. "I guess I haven't given much thought to poetry."

"I have a lot of poetry books in the library. I could show you," she offered.

"I'd like that."

They stood looking at each other for a moment before Sebastian said, "We should keep going. We don't want to lose them."

"Right. You're right, of course. Let's go." Phoebe refused to think about how preposterous it was to believe they could stop the nastiest, scariest, most dangerous brutes the kingdom had ever known. All she wanted was to be with Sebastian for as long as she could, before their adventure—and her excuse for being near him—was over for good.

They followed on through the forest until Phoebe said, "This looks familiar. Isn't this near the dragon's lair?"

"Yes, I recognize it, too. They can't seem to escape their fascination with that dragon."

"But she's never seemed to like them. It's a little late for them to try to make friends, don't you think?"

"Maybe they intend to threaten her into helping them. Or maybe they have some sort of leverage they can use on her."

"I wouldn't want to be threatening a dragon. Would you?"

"Doesn't seem very smart to me. But one thing I know for sure about my father is that he's very smart. So that means he has a plan." *I wish I had one,* Sebastian thought.

Vlad and Boris crossed the charred clearing and paused at the lair's opening, where a campfire was burning low. Phoebe and Sebastian hid nearby, tense and silent, holding each other's hands as they waited to see what would happen.

After a while, the dragon appeared at the mouth of her lair. In the faint light of the campfire, her glittering scales gave off a pearly light. She stood, looking at the Terrible Twos as a stream of gray smoke came from her nostrils.

"We're here to make you an offer you can't refuse," Vlad said. "We're leaving the kingdom for good, and you're coming with us. We'll be so much more in demand in a new location if we bring not only our own well-honed talents, but also our very own dragon." For Boris's benefit, he was saying *we*, but he didn't mean it. He intended to have this dragon all to himself.

The smoke from the dragon's nostrils darkened.

"Oh, I know you've rejected our offers many times in the past," Vlad went on. "But this time we have quite an inducement. His name is Hannibal."

The dragon took a step forward, her gold eyes glowing.

"Yes, indeed. I heard the guards talking about you and the elephant. It's all over the kingdom, thanks to that old blabbermouth, Wendell the wizard. So here's the offer: you come with us and nothing happens to the big guy. You say no again, and we send a p-mail back to our cohort in the stables to put a little something extra in Hannibal's dinner. A little something extra I concocted especially for him in my laboratory. And you know the kind of things that come out of my laboratory."

A look of distress and uncertainty came across the dragon's face.

"Do you think it's true?" Phoebe whispered to Sebastian.

"I don't see how it can be," he whispered back. "He must have made something from all that stuff he always carries in his pockets to allow them to break out of the dungeon, but there's no way he could have left something in the stables. He was taken straight to the dungeon when he arrived, and escaped straight out of the tunnel. He never went to the stables. And he doesn't have a cohort there—at least not anymore. And with all the bad guys banished, he couldn't have planned this while he still had access to a laboratory, since he didn't know he'd be in this situation. He's bluffing all over the place, trying to scare her into coming with them."

"We can't let that happen," Phoebe said. "We can't let them keep doing their terrible deeds." And with that, she stepped forward into the clearing. She was behind the Terrible Twos, but the dragon could see her and issued a stream of white smoke in the shape of a question mark.

"You have questions?" Vlad said. "Well, I have the answers. Don't make a stupid mistake."

The dragon puffed out another question mark.

"Huh?" Boris said. "I don't get it."

"What you don't get"—Phoebe raised her voice—"is that Vlad's *bluffing*. And Sebastian and I know it."

Vlad and Boris spun around.

Phoebe twiddled her fingers at them. "Hi." She looked up at the dragon. "They're bluffing," she said. "They can't do anything to Hannibal. You don't have to do what they want."

"She's right." Sebastian had appeared at her side.

"What are you doing here?" Boris asked. "And who asked you, anyway?"

Vlad didn't bother with questions. He just pulled a handful of his sleeping powder from his pocket and blew it at Phoebe and Sebastian.

Sebastian, who had grown up observing all of Vlad's tricks and had recently been the victim of that very powder, knew what was coming. He yanked Phoebe onto the ground with him before the powder reached them, allowing it to sail harmlessly over their heads—though the spiffle trees it hit keeled right over.

Vlad and Boris ran toward them, fists clenched, ready to do something unspeakable to their very own children. Sebastian rolled over Phoebe, thinking that if he could do nothing else, at least he could protect her.

The dragon's roar filled the forest, and the jet of flame she sent into the night air caused the Terrible Twos to pause in their vicious rush, watching the fire ignite the treetops. Sebastian scrambled to his feet, pulling Phoebe up with him, as the dragon leaped from the mouth of her lair into the clearing. Vlad and Boris turned back to the dragon, who took a few purposeful steps toward them as Phoebe and Sebastian backed away.

With one powerful breath, the dragon aimed a blast of flame at the Terrible Twos.

20

Phoebe and Sebastian were knocked back onto the ground by the gust of fire, their clothes singed by the flames. They helped each other up, rubbing their stinging eyes, coughing, and dusting each other off. As the smoke cleared, they looked around for Vlad and Boris, but all they saw was a big pile of ash in the middle of the clearing.

A gratified-looking dragon was dusting off her front paws.

"Did you . . .?" Sebastian pointed to the ashes.

The dragon nodded with satisfaction.

"Both of them?" Phoebe asked.

Again the dragon nodded.

Phoebe and Sebastian looked at each other. "How do you feel about that?" Sebastian asked.

Phoebe thought for a moment. "I should probably feel worse than I do—after all, Boris was my father—but I'm glad they're gone. Nothing good was ever going to come from them." She looked at Sebastian. "How do *you* feel about it?"

"More complicated than you. Of course I'm glad they can't do any more harm. But I guess I always hoped that in time they would change their ways. That they would become better people." He paused. "And better fathers. Now that possibility is gone forever."

She put her hand on Sebastian's arm. "Did you really think it was a possibility?"

He took a deep breath. "I guess not. I just wanted it."

The dragon had been pacing tentatively back and forth across the clearing, eyeing them uneasily. Phoebe went over and stroked her iridescent neck, telling her, "Okay, so maybe that's not the way we would have planned this. But, to tell you the truth, we didn't have a plan. All we knew is that we had to stop them, but you're the one who did. You also saved people we don't even know from suffering at the hands of the Terrible Twos. They're all very grateful. And so are we."

A tear formed in each of the dragon's eyes, then instantly evaporated into a puff of steam.

As she was comforting the dragon, Phoebe had the odd feeling that she was being watched. Standing on her tiptoes and peering past the dragon's folded shoulder wing, she saw the two women who had been roasting weenies with Marigold standing in the lair's opening. It was hard to tell in the shadows, but they seemed to have tears in their eyes, too.

"Hi," Phoebe said over the dragon. "Sorry you had to see that."

"We're not," the taller one said. "We've waited a long time for it."

"Oh," Phoebe said. "Well, I suppose there are a lot of other people who'd agree with you."

"Our reasons are more personal," the shorter one said.

The other said, "My name is Twyla." She turned to Sebastian. "Did I understand you to say one of those men was your father?"

Not again, Sebastian thought. When would Vlad's

reputation quit following him around? "I'm afraid so," he said.

"Was it Vlad?"

"Yes. And Boris is her father," he said, indicating Phoebe. Maybe he should have let her be the one to reveal her connection to the Terrible Twos if she decided to, but he wanted some company in his predicament.

The shorter woman gasped. "I was afraid to believe my suspicions," she said. "And your name is Phoebe, isn't it?"

Phoebe frowned, puzzled. "How did you know? Did Queen Marigold tell you about me?"

"I know because I'm the one who gave you that name. I'm . . . I'm Anabel. Your mother." Her chin trembled.

"You must be mistaken," Phoebe said. "My mother disappeared long ago. I'm positive she's no longer living or I'm sure she would have been in touch with me." Her own chin trembled. "My mother would never have left me alone with Boris unless something had happened to her. At least I hope she wouldn't."

"Oh, no," Anabel said, twisting her hands together.

"That's not how it happened at all. We'd been so young and unformed when we first married that Boris hadn't yet turned into the monster he would later become. When he did, I was getting ready to run and to take you with me. But he caught me. He said if I wanted to leave so badly, I had to go, but I couldn't take you with me. He'd been a disinterested, neglectful father, so I knew he wanted to keep you only to punish me. And he probably had hopes of influencing you to be like him. And he said if I remained in the kingdom, or ever tried to contact you, he would . . ." She pressed her hand to her mouth. "He would . . . practice his . . . his devices on you. Then I told him I would stay, but he said it was too late, that I'd made my wishes clear and I had to go."

Phoebe gaped at her.

"I see you don't believe me," Anabel said. "What if I told you that I know you have a scar on your elbow from one time when you were playing with one of Boris's forbidden . . . devices . . . and you cut yourself on it? You were just a baby. That was the final straw that convinced me we had to leave."

Phoebe touched her elbow. "Really?"

Anabel nodded. "And Twyla and little Sebastian were going to come with us. Vlad caught them, too. And made the same threat."

"What?" Sebastian said, startled. "You're *my* mother?"

"Yes," Twyla said, nodding at him. "I had to go in a hurry, but I left a book about King Arthur so you would have something from me. And to show you an example of a man unlike your father. Did you find it? Or did Vlad get rid of it? He probably did. There wouldn't be a single thing about King Arthur that he could identify with."

"I found it," Sebastian said faintly. "I always wondered where it came from since, you're right, it certainly wasn't something Vlad would have given me. I must have read it a million times."

"Anabel and I knew we were supposed to leave the kingdom after that, but we just couldn't go that far away from our children. For a while we camped in the forest, picking up scraps of information about you and your fathers from various travelers and hunters passing through. And then we found Winnie." Twyla pointed to the dragon, who lowered her lashes modestly. "She took us in. She was lonely. And she understood about being *mis*understood. What seems to the kingdom to be wanton incineration of acres of the forest happens only in the spring, when all the blooming flowers and grasses cause her allergies to act up. She's actually in very good control of her fire-breathing—I think you just witnessed some of that precision—except when she sneezes. Then flames just come shooting out of her nostrils. She can't help it. And she's always been ashamed and embarrassed about it."

"She's protected and cared for us for years," Anabel said. "That allowed us to stay near you, even if we couldn't be close enough to see you. We worried all the time that your fathers were either hurting you or turning you into dangerous people, like themselves. From what we've seen just now, though, we think you've both turned out remarkably well. We're very proud of you."

Phoebe and Sebastian were speechless with astonishment.

"I know this is a lot to digest," Twyla said. "Maybe you should sleep on it. Think about what you want to do."

Phoebe and Sebastian nodded in unison. Their

heads were too full to fit even one more thought. In the past three days, they had been involved in a kidnapping plot, gone without sleep, walked for miles, learned even more terrible things about their fathers, lost their fathers, found their mothers, and probably begun to fall into hopeless love. They needed a breather.

"You could come back to the castle with us," Phoebe said. "It's safe to do that now."

Anabel and Twyla looked at each other, then at Winnie, and then back to each other.

"Oh," Phoebe said. "Of course. Well, what the heck. Bring her, too. I think Hannibal would like that. And maybe the court physician can do something about the allergies. Or Wendell can."

"Excuse us for a minute," Twyla said. The women drew away and spent a few minutes in furious whispering before they returned and Anabel said, "I think we'll wait here. You two need time to absorb all this. And so do we. Let's not make any hasty decisions. Come back once you've had a chance to weigh everything."

After saying their goodbyes, an exhausted Phoebe and Sebastian headed back through the dark forest to the castle.

"I'm relieved we have time to think," Phoebe said. "Aren't you?"

"I'm too tired to even think about thinking," he said. "And too . . . For once I don't know what the right word is. *Surprised* isn't enough. *Overwhelmed* is too mild. *Gobsmacked* may be the right one."

Gobsmacked, Phoebe thought. *Perfect.*

As they approached the Zandelphia-Beaurivage Bridge and saw the castle on the other side, they noticed a lot of torchlight and clamorous noise.

"I guess they've noticed the Terrible Twos are gone," Phoebe said.

"Goner than they know," Sebastian said.

The closer they came to the castle, the louder the noise grew and the more people they saw running back and forth on the terrace and among the battlements.

"We're going to have a lot of explaining to do," Sebastian said. "Are you up for it?"

"As long as you're with me while we do it."

He smiled and took her hand. As long as he was too tired to think, he relied on his feelings. And they said, *Take her hand and don't let go.* "I will be."

21

By the time they were finished explaining what had happened since Sebastian witnessed the Terrible Twos escaping from the dungeon, they were just about incoherent with fatigue. Phoebe had slumped over onto the large round table in the throne room, her head on her arms, her eyes closed. Every time Rollo or Chris or Marigold asked her a question, Sebastian had to shake her to wake her up.

"We've got the whole story by now," Chris said. "Let's all go get some sleep."

Phoebe lifted her head. "I forgot to ask. About Poppy." Her voice wavered.

"We can wake her up now—though she just falls

back to sleep," Marigold said. "The doctor says the sleeping potion will wear off soon. Mrs. Sunday's keeping a close eye on her. Our princess will be fine."

Phoebe wobbled as she stood up. "I'm so glad."

"Go," Marigold said. "Get some sleep. And you know we'll never be able to thank you."

"We can talk about bringing the dragon in later," Sebastian said as he and Phoebe headed for the door.

"About what?" Chris asked.

"Good night," Sebastian said, then closed the door.

A whole day passed before Phoebe and Sebastian were awake again. Sebastian came to the library, where Phoebe was sitting at her desk, doing nothing.

"How are you?" he asked tentatively.

"All right. Sleep helps. How about you?" He looked so good to her, all washed and brushed and dressed in clean clothes. The last time she'd seen him, he'd been dirty and red-eyed and disheveled. And he'd looked good to her even then.

"All right. I went to the blacksmith shop to see if I still had a job, but Maurice told me the king had said I could have all the days off I wanted. And Maurice was nicer to me than he's ever been. I guess being associated with the royal family instead of the Terrible Twos makes a difference." His voice had a trace of bitterness.

"I know what you mean. It's happening to me, too. Already today I've had more people come in to get books and have a look at me than normally come into the library in a week." She shrugged. "Of course, they should always have been judging us on our own qualities. But they weren't."

"And they're *still* not!" Sebastian said.

"But isn't it better like that? This way they'll spend more time with us and that will let them see who we are."

"But it's not fair. It's wrong." Sebastian slumped onto a stool and ran his fingers through his hair. "We're still just a curiosity to everyone in the kingdom."

Phoebe came over and stood behind his stool, then put her arms around him. The strange happenings—the chase through the forest, Winnie's intervention, the discovery of lost mothers—had somehow freed her. If she'd learned nothing else, it was that life was unpredictable, to put it mildly. Hanging on to whatever might help one survive the bombshells seemed the sanest thing to do. Besides, she thought Sebastian was wonderful—brave and smart and gallant in the face of his personal trials and disappointments.

She would have to be certifiable to let all that get away if she could help it. "You're right," she said. "It's not fair. What should we do about it?"

"Do? What can we do? That's just the way people are." Sebastian wasn't so far gone that he couldn't appreciate how soft Phoebe's arms around him were and how good she smelled. And how surprised he was to have her so close. He was certainly capable of judging those qualities of hers.

"You're right again," she said, hugging him harder. "That *is* just how people are. The way I see it, the only thing we can do is to try not to be that way ourselves. What do you say we start with Winnie? Everybody thinks she's awful and dangerous because of her flames, but we know differently. So we have to treat her differently. And we have to let everyone know about her allergies."

Sebastian stood and faced Phoebe, then stepped past the stool and put his arms around her. She was just as soft and smelled just as good when he was standing as when he was sitting. "You're right, too," he said, holding her close. "We've got to go to the king and convince him it would be safe for her to live at the castle." Then, remembering the great blast of flame that had torched the Terrible Twos, he added, "Or maybe live slightly closer to the castle."

"Or maybe the thing to do is to move Hannibal," Phoebe suggested. "He's bored here, and he makes the unicorns nervous. He'd be happier living out in the forest with Winnie, don't you think?"

Sebastian held her closer. "Brilliant. We should tell the king."

And after quite a while, which included locking the door to the library, they did.

"It sounds fine to me," Chris told them. "But we have to ask Wendell. He and Hannibal have been together a long time."

At that moment, Swithbert, Ed, and Wendell came into the throne room.

"Where's that granddaughter of mine?" Swithbert

said. "Is what those vermin did to her all cured now? Is she waking up the way she should be?"

Chris smiled and gestured to the cradle, from which issued a series of happy cooing sounds. Swithbert picked up the baby and they cooed at each other.

Ed said, "I can tell you, when we heard that baby was going to be all right, there wasn't a dry seat in the castle."

"I'm so happy to hear that," Marigold said. "I think."

"Wendell," Chris said. "You're just the man we need to see."

"Me?" Wendell asked nervously. "I thought everything was all good now."

"Sebastian has a proposition he wants to run by you," Chris said. "Go for it, Sebastian."

So, with great ardor, Sebastian made the case for letting Hannibal move into the forest with Winnie. Once Wendell had heard him out, he replied, "You're right."

Sebastian was a bit taken aback at having been found right so many times in one day. And so easily.

"I've been worried about Hannibal for quite a while,"

Wendell went on. "I may be retired from wizardry and liking it, but he's just bored. And it's not kind to keep him shut up in the stables so much of the time. He's begun to suffer a bit from ennui. I know he likes Winnie, and he'd love having a whole big forest to roam around in. How can I say no?"

"Good," Chris said. "So that's taken care of. Now, about Anabel and Twyla."

"I don't know much about them yet," Phoebe said. "But I do know they shouldn't be assumed to be like the husbands they ran away from and haven't seen in years. It's not fair. Right, Sebastian?" He nodded and she continued. "And I liked very much how they didn't force a response from us, or insist on coming back to the castle with us, even after all those years of living in Winnie's lair. It means they were thinking of us before themselves. Would it be all right if they moved back here if they want to?"

"I see no reason why not," Marigold said. "And now that Winnie will have company, they won't worry about her. Do you think they'd want to come back?"

"I suppose the only way to find out is to ask them," Phoebe said practically.

"Would you prefer if I did that?" Marigold asked. "If they're unsure, it might be less awkward for you and easier for them."

"Thank you, Your Highness," Phoebe said, relieved.

"You can call me Marigold. I'm not all that high."

They giggled together.

"Now it's my turn," Swithbert said, handing Poppy back to Marigold. "I, too, have a proposition. I want to adopt a couple more children."

"Papa!" Marigold cried. "What made you think of that? You've already raised me and my sisters."

"Well, having a father is important, don't you think? Mothers are fine—most of them, anyway—but fathers are special." He held up his hand to prevent Marigold from butting in. "That's not just ego talking, though I think I was a pretty good one, so maybe it *is* ego talking. Every kid needs a father."

"You make a good point, Swithbert," Chris said. "Do you have any particular children in mind?"

"Yes, I do. I'd like to adopt Phoebe and Sebastian."

You wouldn't think jaws falling open would make such a loud sound, but when a lot of them do it all at once, it's quite an event. Undeterred, Swithbert went on. "These two young people have shown courage and fortitude in dealing with the circumstances of their families, in spite of some terrible and/or absent parenting. They've become sensational citizens. They saved Poppy. They participated in the elimination of the Terrible Twos. And they haven't asked for a thing in return except for someone else."

"For Hannibal," Wendell added. "And for Winnie, too. And for their mothers."

"I think they should be rewarded," Swithbert said. "You can give them whatever you want, Chris, but these kids have earned having a good dad for a change. So, what do you think?"

A lot of jaws closing at the same time make another interesting sound.

"Don't you think you should ask Phoebe and Sebastian what *they* think?" Christian asked.

Swithbert turned to them. "Well?"

Sebastian was the first to speak. "But that means we'll be brother and sister, doesn't it?"

It took a moment, but Swithbert got it. "Oh. I see. Yes. That would be awkward. All right. How would you like to have a doting, adoptive *uncle*?"

Phoebe stepped forward. The surprises were coming so fast, she could barely keep up with them, but she had already learned that the best response to bad surprises was strength, and to good ones, gratitude. So she said, "Would it be okay if I hugged my Uncle Swithbert?"

Swithbert beamed and accepted the hug, which was followed by one from Sebastian.

"Now, Swithbert," Chris said, "you make another good point about rewards. I have something I'd like to say about that." He beckoned Sebastian to him. When Sebastian started to kneel at Christian's feet, Chris stopped him. "I may be a king," he said. "But even kings need friends, and I'd like you to be mine."

"Me?" Sebastian asked, stunned.

Chris nodded. "I appreciate your active mind, your good instincts, and your competence. And I know you're the one who makes those terrific Camelot miniatures for that stall on Market Day. Maurice showed me your workshop, where you think he doesn't know what you're making. But I also know why you're so interested in King Arthur and his knights."

Sebastian swallowed. "You do?"

"Yes. And I admire that, too. With a father like yours, it makes perfect sense that you would look for a better role model. And you picked the best. I try to emulate him myself, even though I had a very good father. And to show you that I believe you've succeeded in becoming the exact opposite of Vlad, I'm going to knight you. Now you can kneel, Sir Sebastian."

Sebastian knelt, and it was a good thing, too; he was so astounded, he wasn't sure his legs would continue to support him. After the tap of Christian's sword on his shoulders, he didn't really feel any different inside, but it was impossible for him to quit smiling. He stood and bowed to the man who was both his king and his friend. "Thank you, sire."

"Call me Chris. We're going to be spending a lot of time together now, you know. I want you to show me how to make one of those Arthurian maces. And as good as your King Arthur models are, I bet we can think of some other interesting things to put together from that pile of scraps in your workshop. Now, as for you, Phoebe . . ."

"Me?" Phoebe squeaked.

"Yes, you. Sebastian's not the only one who's overcome a questionable upbringing."

"Questionable?" Marigold interrupted indignantly. "How about rotten? Neglectful? Cruel?"

"All right," Chris said. "All of those. Anyway, Phoebe, I'll knight you, too, if you like, but I think I know of something you'd rather have."

"You do?" Phoebe asked.

"Yes. I'm going to set you up with Magnus, the court architect, so the two of you can design exactly the manor house you'd like to live in. And then I'm going to see that it gets built for you."

Phoebe burst into tears—and was quickly gathered into the arms of her brand-new uncle.

"She means 'thank you,'" Swithbert translated.

"I get it," Chris said. "Now, what do you say we all go get some lunch and hope nothing else exciting happens today."

Ed said, beaming at everyone, "It's a good day when you can get two birds stoned at once."

22

For the next four weeks, everybody in the castle worked like beavers to get ready for Poppy's Welcome Party. The seamstresses sewed up party dresses, table-cloths, and new draperies. The carpenters built arbors and dining tables, bleacher seats and barstools. The gardeners dug and watered, raked and hoed.

And Chris and Marigold labored to get the trials of Emlyn, Fogarty, and Bartholomew settled so that they could enjoy the festivities without that hanging over their heads.

Bartholomew's sentence was easy. He was so abjectly contrite and remorseful about his part in the kidnapping that punishment was hardly necessary. Instead, Chris and Marigold assigned him to a period of working on Magnus's estate, just so Bartholomew could observe how a good man conducts himself. Bartholomew's main problem was that he had lacked a role model for courageous conduct. Chris was making sure that he got one. And Magnus was more flattered than he could say, since he himself had once suffered from a lack of good examples. Only with the help of his darling wife, Sephronia, and the forgiveness of Christian and Marigold had he been able to live down his shameful conduct as an admittedly reluctant cohort of Queen Olympia. His atonement was to be the finest man he could possibly be, forever.

Emlyn and Fogarty were more of a problem. They were recalcitrant to the point of foolishness, denying that they had anything to do with the kidnapping, despite evidence—including Mrs. Sunday's eyewitness testimony—to the contrary. They insisted that everything that had happened was some sort of misunderstanding or mistake or distortion. It is very hard to be sensible with people who are anything but.

In the end, Marigold and Chris decided, as much as it pained them to do so, that it was best to leave Emlyn and Fogarty in the dungeon until they became curious about what punishment they could get if they came clean. Time spent in that dungeon could make one think that almost any other kind of punishment would be preferable. What form that would take would be something the king and queen figured out once things at the palace settled down again.

In the meantime, Chris and Marigold found time to spend many hours with Poppy and to watch a companionable relationship develop between Poppy's goat (whom they had named Tallulah) and all the dogs, especially Bub. Tallulah followed Bub everywhere and he, to their surprise, seemed not to mind. Admiration, even from an unlikely source, is a tonic for anyone.

Marigold put Wendell and the court physician to work finding a remedy for Winnie's allergies, and they seemed to be making some progress: the incidence of sneeze-induced conflagrations was decreasing. Winnie and Marigold had also begun a p-mail correspondence in which they swapped elephant jokes. Hannibal knew every one that had ever been told—there were quite a lot of them—and he was happy to share with Winnie. In the way of communication they had devised over the years, Winnie passed them along to Anabel or Twyla, who p-mailed them to the queen. Marigold's current favorite was "What's gray and wrinkly and jumps every twenty seconds? An elephant with hiccups."

The only blight on the days leading up to the big party had to do with the rivalry between Swithbert and Wendell for Mrs. Clover's affections. It seemed that she and Denby, Swithbert's valet, had been sweethearts for a long time but had kept it a secret for fear of being found guilty of inappropriate workplace behavior (as well as making a king mad—while Swithbert was still king). But once Marigold and Christian found out about their romance and assured them that there was nothing illegal or inappropriate about it, they came out in the open with their love.

This caused Swithbert and Wendell to spend a lot of time in the ale shop over *venti*-size tankards of mead, drowning their sorrows and commiserating about the fickleness of women—although as Ed (newly and happily married to the red-haired troll Wendolyn) kept reminding them, if someone doesn't want to be with you, nobody can stop them.

With everything else on her mind, Marigold still

found time to worry about the welcome gifts the fairies would bring to her little girl. Poppy had already gotten off to a rather bumpy start, and Marigold didn't want any more bumps for her for a very long time. But there wasn't much she could do about it except hope Wendell could be helpful if something magical started going awry.

Finally the day of the big blowout arrived, and all the guests were crammed into every corner of the castle.

The court crier had made himself hoarse with all the announcements generated by such a big crowd. There had been several fistfights to report, usually for romantic reasons; a few accidental falls down the castle stairs, usually the result of too much celebrating; one case of mistaken identity, with embarrassing results; lots of scheduling changes; all the details of the business of the Terrible Twos, and Hannibal and Winnie the dragon; Swithbert's new status as uncle to Sebastian and Phoebe; and several elephant jokes, as commanded by Queen Marigold, who thought all the guests would appreciate them. (What's big and gray with horns? An elephant marching band. Why do elephants have trunks? They would look funny with suitcases. What is beautiful, gray, and wears glass slippers? Cinderelephant. The real Cinderella, who was a Welcome Party guest, was not amused.)

Christian's brothers and Marigold's sisters had arrived from their own kingdoms; old friends Mr. Lucasa (now known as Santa Claus), Susan (once called Lazy Susan), and Angelica (loosely related to Queen Olympia) had come from the North Pole. Mrs. Clover had done an excellent job of assigning guest rooms so that no feuding parties were even on the same floor, and all valets and ladies' maids were quartered within hollering distance of those they served. The footmen were taking bets on which lady in waiting would have the first hissy fit.

The corridors bustled with overdressed countesses, foppish barons, fairies trailing glittering magic dust, and pageboys dashing along with urgent messages. The kitchens were in operation night and day delivering delicacies at all hours and doing their best to satisfy exotic tastes. Who would have guessed there would be such a demand for medallions of hedgehog in rhubarb-dandelion sauce?

The castle was filled with flowers and candles and various sweetmeats, and after several days of pandemonium, the long-awaited festivities were just moments away.

Bub and Cate, and Flopsy, Mopsy, and Topsy had retreated under the bed in Marigold and Christian's suite, but not—this time—because they were pouting. Marigold had wanted to include them and show them off, to the point of bathing them all in perfumed shampoo and decking them out with fancy collars and ribbons. But as much as Cate loved a party, she had been stepped on one time too many by the hordes of guests. And the other dogs had been to enough parties that they didn't care if they never got to another. The spilled food to lick up was not enough to compensate for all the times a guest wiped his hands on them, or some child pulled their tails or ears, or someone kicked them under a table. They knew Marigold would bring them a generous sampling of the goodies, which was the best part of a party, anyway, so they were happy to remain out of the way now that they knew they were part of the family again.

* * *

It was a sparkling spring day, and all the guests had finally gathered on the terrace. Poppy, dressed in purple and yellow, with a minimum of ruffles and bows, was wheeled under the bower in her cradle, wide-eyed and alert. She'd never seen such a crowd, and once she understood that she was the main attraction, she laughed and clapped her chubby little hands. When the audience laughed and clapped back, she had her first experience of relating to her future subjects. It was quite a congenial moment, which boded well for the life of the kingdom. Poppy also loved getting all dressed up and hoped there would be lots more occasions when that would be expected, especially if they were occasions she could share with her favorite people (her papa and her mama, her two grandfathers, her dogs, her goat, and her nanny), all of whom she could see from where she sat propped against purple and yellow pillows.

King Christian stood next to the cradle, ready to welcome the assemblage. He waited until the loud hum of conversation simmered down, and was especially grateful when the high-pitched and competitive twittering of all the fairies ceased. Their shrill voices almost always gave him a headache.

"Queen Marigold and I thank you all for joining with us to welcome our little princess, Poppy, into the world," he began. "We are confident that you will all be available to help us guide her to be a responsible and productive citizen, and a conscientious princess to her kingdom." He went on with equal parts flattery and sincerity until he could no longer postpone the time he knew Marigold dreaded—the bestowal of the fairy gifts.

The first few were traditional: silver cups, good health, ivory rattles, kindness. But then came trouble. A fairy who had had insomnia most of her life began to bestow the gift of good sleep.

When formerly–Lazy Susan, sitting in the audience, heard that, she jumped to her feet. There had been a time in her life when uninterrupted naps were all she wanted, but that was before she had learned the pleasures of absorbing and satisfying work. Besides, through her half sister, Sleeping Beauty, she knew more than almost anybody about the opposite of insomnia.

"Whoa," she said. "I'm so sorry to interrupt," she added, remembering her manners. "But perhaps you recall that my half sister is Sleeping Beauty, so maybe I'm a little oversensitive, but this one makes me nervous. Just a little too much and . . . well, eight hours of sleep is good. Twenty hours is a problem. Don't you think? And don't forget about Vlad's sleeping powder. Sleep is a sensitive issue around here." Abruptly she sat down.

The crowd hushed in shock. They had never heard anyone object to a fairy gift before, though there were definitely times when someone should have.

The fairy was glowering, hands on her hips, clenching a wand that could do unpredictable damage.

Marigold stepped forward, hoping she had enough tact to handle this. "Thank you very much, Prilla, for this lovely gift," she said. "I'm sure every new parent would wish for it, when their babies are waking up several times a night. Um . . . how hard is it to make sure the gift is exactly eight hours?"

Poppy was surprised to hear that her nighttime waking was a problem. She had been so happy every time her mommy appeared that she naturally assumed these visits had been as pleasant for Mommy as for herself. That's one reason she had done it so often.

Prilla shook her wand and a few sparkles fell onto the terrace. "It is a great art," she grumped.

"I understand," said Marigold, who really didn't. "Do you mind if I have our resident wizard emeritus observe? I think he would be very interested in your technique." She turned to where Wendell sat in the front row and said through clenched teeth, *"Wouldn't you, Wendell?"*

Wendell got the message and unfurled his own wand from under his robes. "Indeed," he said, joining Prilla and the royal family under the arbor. He hoped he still had enough of his wizarding mojo to alter Prilla's gift if it appeared to be excessive.

Prilla waved her wand in a series of maneuvers that were so fast, they began to blur. But Wendell had been at this game a lot longer than she had, and he could follow the pattern enough to see that she was loading Poppy up with several hours too many. With a few minor twitches of his own wand, he was able to recalibrate the gift so that it settled in at exactly eight hours and forty-seven minutes. When all the wand action was finished, a shower of rainbow-colored spangles fell around the cradle, settled on Poppy's blanket and pillow, and fizzled out.

"Thank you very much for this learning opportunity," Marigold told Prilla. "Right, Wendell?" She gave him a subtle poke in the ribs.

"Ow! Yes, yes, of course," he said. "Very nice opportunity."

Prilla gave a smug bow to the audience and flitted back to her seat.

The rest of the gifts were problem free, though Marigold kept Wendell within reach, to ensure there were no more glitches.

Just as the last gift had been presented, there was the sound of a great flapping of wings and a long shadow fell over the terrace. Looking up, the guests were startled by the dazzling sight of an iridescent dragon flying back and forth above them, the sunlight bouncing blindingly off her silvery scales.

Marigold looked up and waved. At that, Winnie opened her claw and dropped a package wrapped in layers of the softest feather moss. It hit the terrace and rolled to the foot of the cradle as Winnie flapped away.

Marigold picked up the bundle and pulled away the wrappings. Inside was a diamond as big as Poppy's head. And it had been shaped, by claw and by fiery breath, into an image of Poppy's face.

"Oh, my," Marigold said. "I knew Winnie's lair was studded with diamonds—they gave it such a pretty light inside—but I had no idea she could do *this* with them. She's a genius!"

"I think she's got a career in lapidary art opening up for herself," Chris said. "If she wants it."

After that, the revelry, gluttony, and debauchery set in in earnest, and it was three days and three nights (in each of which Poppy slept exactly eight hours and forty-seven minutes) more before the guests began packing up to go home.

For Phoebe and Sebastian, those three days were unlike any either of them had ever experienced. For one thing, people who had previously ignored or scorned them could now hardly resist seeking them out for praise or invitations or general sucking up. It was hard for them not to feel some satisfaction at this change of affairs, but they also knew how superficial it was, and how temporary it could be.

From each other they had learned how a *true* friend behaves: steadily there in good times and bad; valuing the other, but not being afraid to offer correction and guidance when necessary; available for extensive hanging out, which can sometimes be more fun than an elaborate planned event.

From time to time they needed to seek out the quiet of the deserted library for a respite from all the merrymaking and fawning. On the afternoon of the second day, Sebastian asked, "How are you holding up? We've had a lot of changes in a short time."

"I don't know if I could get through it alone. I mean, without you. I'm glad I don't have to."

"Thank you. I feel the same way. And not just because we experienced similar childhoods."

"I know. It's more than that." She paused. "Did you know that all porcupines float?" Then, her anxiety momentarily relieved, she went on. "I like you better than anyone else I have ever known." She looked down at her hands in her lap, her cheeks flushed from her daring. Sebastian knelt before her and took her hands into his.

"I was about to say the same thing," he said. "And, no, I didn't know porcupines could float."

"Oh." Her cheeks flushed redder. "Did you know I can cut a thousand strips of p-mail paper in half an hour with my wonderful new p-mail paper cutter?"

"No, but I'm glad. That was my goal when I invented it."

"You invented it?" She looked up to see him gazing at her with the same expression King Christian had had on his face when he'd found Queen Marigold safely outside Winnie's lair: as if no one else existed.

He nodded.

"Thank you," she whispered.

"You're welcome," he whispered back, taking her into his arms and kissing her.

When she could breathe again, Phoebe said, "Did you know yaks give pink milk?"

"What's a yak?" Sebastian asked.

"I can't believe I know a word you don't," she said. And he kissed her again. Sometimes words aren't the most important things going on.

After a while they talked about their mothers, who would be moving into the castle after the festivities were over. Anabel and Twyla had decided that they wanted a calmer atmosphere than the Welcome Party in which to get reacquainted with Phoebe and Sebastian.

"Are you afraid you won't like your mother?" Sebastian asked.

"I already like her," Phoebe said. "I like how she wanted to take me with her when she ran away, and how she stayed as close as she could, and how she wanted to wait to come back here so she wouldn't be putting pressure on me. Why? Are you afraid you won't like yours?"

"I don't think so. It's just odd to think about having a parent I like, and can talk to, and am not afraid of."

"I understand that. I'll help you. If you'll help me."

He kissed her again.

Who needs a party, even if it has jugglers and dancing bears and fireworks?

23

IN THE WEEKS AFTER the Welcome Party, spring came in earnest. Sunlight poured down onto the kingdom. The baffer-birds sang their hearts out. Winnie soared lazily through the azure skies, looking down on the royal family and her best pal, Hannibal. And peace settled over them all like a blanket of feather moss.

It probably wouldn't last. It never does. But it would come back around again. That's how life works. And that's why it's important to treasure the peaceful times—so you can persevere through the other kind.

Carpe diem ever after.